HUNG *Up*

Book design and cover art by Sierra Mac

ISBN 979-8-9954753-0-9

Self published by Sierra Mac

For Grandma Debbie,
My reading addiction started at a young age because of you. You would have been so proud of me for writing my book. I hope you're reading it now with your toes in the sand and the sun on your face.

And for those who are also missing someone who encouraged you to read, to write, or go after your dreams…this is for you.

HUNG *Up*

SIERRA MAC

READER NOTE

Hung Up is a small-town, slow-burn cowgirl romance. It ultimately is meant to be a fun read. However, there may be subjects throughout this book that may be triggering for some.

Explicit language

Near death experience

Explicit sex scenes

Emotional manipulation

Fear, trauma, and anxiety

Alcohol consumption

Mentions infertility

Main character says *no* to sex but ultimately gives in to her ex. The experience hurts her emotionally

HUNG *Up*

1

SORREL

As a barrel racer, nothing matches the high I get charging down a sixty-foot alleyway on horseback at top speed. I imagine I feel the same way about barrel racing as drug addicts do about crack. I'm darn right addicted.

Today that sensation is no different when we emerge into the arena. The lights are bright, and I pray the ground is good. It's just me and Zip. The rest of the world goes dark. I don't hear the announcer saying my name or the roar of the crowd. The only thing I make out is the sound of hooves pounding into the deep arena dirt and Zip's heavy breaths as he runs his heart out for me.

As I turn the first barrel to the right, my foot almost taps it—I miss it by mere centimeters. We're wicked fast moving to the second.

God, I love this. My soul craves it.

In seconds I'm in position to turn the last barrel. I sit deep in my seat and I grab the horn of the saddle with my right hand, gripping the reins in my left. We turn as smooth as leather soles on a hardwood dance floor. Zip digs his hooves into the dirt and curves his muscular body left around the barrel. It's a clean turn. He opens up, stretching out his long powerful legs. I push him hard running home, possibly setting a record time.

Once we're almost to the alleyway, that's when it hits me—the noise. The crowd is going crazy. I'm smiling from ear to ear as we clear the arena. I pull up on the reins to slow him down before getting to the end of the breezeway, and we come to a slow trot.

I finally let out a breath. Leaning down, I stroke Zip's neck, so proud of my young barrel horse. Scoring a fast time of 16.97 seconds, my jaw damn near falls to the floor. Holy fuck.

It's been so long since I've had anything remotely close to a good run, and we probably just ended up winning the whole damn thing. Divine intervention was definitely at play. I had been praying like a cowboy caught in a lightning storm.

Unwrapping Zip's legs and loosening his cinch, I walk him around the arena grounds. I let him stretch his legs and cool off. There's frothy sweat all over his chestnut-colored hair. I look him over with a smile I can't seem to get rid of.

"You sure were working hard, my little Zipper," I tell him like he can understand me. His ears twitch so I know he's listening.

Continuing our walk, I turn through the first row of trailers. I keep my eyes peeled for a black Dodge

Dually with a white camper on the bed. I'm sure he's probably parked on the other side of the rodeo grounds with the roughies, but I keep scanning the rigs just in case.

The roughies travel in a different kind of setup so they're easy to spot. No need for a horse trailer since the stock contractors own the bucking horses and bulls. Bronc riders and bull riders can show up with their gear. Most of them sleep in their car half the time. I think of them more like the hippies of the rodeo world, free spirits going wherever the wind takes them. Barrel racers on the other hand are complete opposites. We have trucks, trailers, semis, you name it. We always show up with more than enough horses—usually, a pack full of dogs too.

Walking down the second row of trailers, we pass Bloomers, Lakota's, and Platinums. There's some nice rigs out here today—that's a pro rodeo for you.

We're almost to the back row now and I spot my rig. A modest setup, but still more than enough for just me and two horses, no doubt. I purposefully parked toward the back so I could peel out after my run—it was also easier to hide out in the back. I managed to steer clear of my ex all weekend. I'm over worrying about running into him at rodeos. I haven't entered half of the rodeos I normally do in the summer. And if I was being honest, I spent most of it hiding out at the ranch. I've been able to avoid him since our breakup. I got lucky. He was in Arizona all winter and busy with rodeo season here most of the summer.

When I skimmed the bronc riding entries before

my run, my heart sank into the pit of my gut. There it was, fifth from the top. *Huck Kenzington.* There should be a damn red flag printed next to his name. Hell, it might save a buckle bunny a little heartbreak. Bless their hearts, not knowing any better—most cowgirls do. Well, except me, I guess…I thought I did, but I wasn't thinking right in the heat of the moment. Got swept up in the intensity of it all. Now everyone and their mothers know we broke up. Of course, they would though. That's what happens when you live in small-town Montana. Everyone knows everything about everybody. Being on the rodeo circuit doesn't help either—it's like being on a reality TV show. There's always some kind of gossip and drama going on somewhere. Huck and I were the entertainment of the year.

Zip whinnies at Duke, tied up to the trailer.

"Hey, bud," I say to Duke, as I tie Zip up next to him. "We did it! We finally won a check. Now I can afford the entry fees from this weekend and your bag of grain," I joke, roughing Duke's forelock.

I decided to run Zip last minute this weekend. I was happy with my choice. Duke is my best barrel horse, but he seemed off lately. I couldn't put my finger on it. Zip is young—he's had plenty of wet saddle pads, but this was his first professional rodeo. I'd say he more than proved he's ready today.

I train all of my barrel horses. My mom taught me everything she knew about barrel racing and training horses. She rode with me in her belly until she couldn't anymore. The first time she ever put me on a horse was when I was two years old. I entered my first race at four and haven't given it up since.

As I open the door to my trailer, my dachshund Dash comes running out. His tiny little legs are moving as fast as they can. Barrel racers get a lot of shit for the dogs we choose, most of them being wiener dogs, corgis, or any type of cattle dog breed. Maybe it's because they're kinda like barrel racers—a little crazy, a whole lot of fierceness, and tons of attitude packed into a tiny little body. Until you own one, you wouldn't get it.

I'm eager to get back home as I load up my gear. "Time to load up, guys," I say, to the horses.

If I were quick about it, I could be on the road this evening and back to the ranch by sunset. I move faster, emptying water buckets and mucking the horses' portable pens. I hear footsteps approaching and look up to see my best friend Charli headed toward my trailer. I never responded to her text earlier about going to some concert tonight they're having at the rodeo grounds. I groan internally. Hopefully she'll notice I'm packed up and ready to leave and let me off the hook tonight.

She struts over, her honey-brown curls bobbing up and down, and a smirk on her lips. *Here we go*, I think.

"Sorrel Saxxon, where on earth do you think you're going? You aren't leaving now, are you?" she says with her southern drawl.

Charli steps in front of me and puts her hands on her hips. She's only about five feet tall with a short, curvy frame. Her cowboy hat gives her an extra inch, but I still tower over her.

"Charli, I told you before your run, I need to get back to the ranch tonight. We're moving cattle in the morning and Dad needs my help."

She flips her hair back over her shoulder and crosses her arms. "Oh, come on, Sorrel, you know damn well your daddy has more than enough hands. Stay one more night. You could use a little fun," she says, raising an eyebrow.

I bite back a smile. It's so hard to say no to her. She could convince a mule to listen to her, and they're about as stubborn as it gets.

Charli is originally from Texas but moved to Montana when we were in high school, where she lived with us until we graduated. I've known her most of my life since our moms barrel raced together.

She was hanging with a rough crowd in Texas, and her mom thought it would be a good idea for her to live here. There isn't much trouble to get into when you're on a ranch fifty miles from the closest town. Dad calls her a little fireball made up of 90 percent attitude and 10 percent caffeine. We love her. She makes life fun.

I groan and throw my head back. "Charli, please don't make me stay." I have a habit of giving in to her.

She gives me a grin, knowing she's already won the battle. I walk over to Zip still tied to the trailer. I bend down and clean his feet out so I can put him in his portable pen. I guess I won't be loading him into the trailer. Good thing I didn't take the pens down yet.

I'm buying time even though I'm going to tell her I'll stay. She starts tapping her foot impatiently.

"Fine, one more night," I say.

She claps her hands in celebration while walking away backward, still eyeing me.

"I'll be back in an hour. Get your ass ready and you better look hot when I get back," she demands.

Saluting her with two fingers, I say, "Yes, ma'am."

I'm longing to get back to the ranch. But I guess one more night won't kill me.

Our ranch has been in my family for eight generations. It spans across thirty-three thousand acres throughout the Pryor Mountains with some of the most stunning views in all of Montana. My role is handling the financial aspects, such as bookkeeping. When I'm not in the office, I help the ranch hands from time to time, but my major project now is the guest portion of our ranch. Or what some might call a "dude ranch." We don't call it that though because more than anything the Saxxon Ranch is a full working ranch. Dad runs the guest portion when I'm gone. My oldest sister Sutton and her husband Ryder manage most of the operation. Ranching is what they love to do and they hardly ever leave the ranch.

Sutton never got into rodeo as much as me and my youngest sister Sable, so she had a lot more time to work on the ranch and learn the ins and outs. She didn't like barrel racing, said there was too much drama, and she wasn't wrong about that.

Sable did breakaway roping when we were kids and throughout high school, but nowadays she doesn't rodeo much at all. Last year she moved to Billings with Mom. She enrolled in a few courses at the university and said she wanted to live in the city for a while. We all miss her so much, but I have a feeling she'll be back eventually.

I sure as hell would never live in the city. The only reason I ever go to Billings is to visit Mom and Sable or for business. The ranch is my favorite place in the world. If I'm not on the road rodeoing, there isn't much that can call me away.

I finish putting the horses up, and I look down at my watch to see I only have thirty minutes left until Charli is back. When I look up, I see the silhouette of a tall cowboy in all black and my heart feels like it's going to run out of my chest. I make a run for my trailer and sink into the closed door with relief when I'm safely inside, double checking to make sure the door is locked.

2

SORREL

I move through the living quarters of my horse trailer like a mad woman as I get ready. Space is tight, and it's hard to keep organized, but it's my home away from home. I've made it as cozy as can be, but it's not nearly as cozy as my cabin back at the ranch.

I rinse off the arena dirt and sweat sticking to my neck and face. It's been a long day, and between the heat and my nerves from earlier, I'm a hot mess. I throw on some makeup, a clean pair of jeans, and a baby-pink tank top. Next, I work on the rat's nest that's my hair. My braid came undone during my run, and my hair is all tangled. I start at the bottom brushing through my long blonde hair. I work at the knots until it's smooth.

I'm a natural toe-head blonde—been that way since I was a kid. I stick out like a sore thumb compared to my sisters. I've always found it ironic I was named Sorrel, considering it was after my mom's favorite sorrel horse. I'm pretty sure my parents were just trying to think of unique names starting with *S*. They admitted to having more boy *S* names picked out in hopes at least one of us would come out a little cowboy. But after the third girl, they gave up on trying for a boy.

Dad realized he would just have to raise us to be tough enough to work on the ranch, and he did just that. Each of us girls is as handy as the ranch hands that are hired. Especially Sutton. She's as gritty as they come and one of the hardest workers I know. But I think Sable would prefer not to work at all if were up to her. It's not that she isn't handy, but she enjoys doing her makeup and shopping more than she enjoys ranch work. I think I fall somewhere in the middle.

Dad finally got his boy of the family when Sutton and Ryder had their baby boy, Trotter. I'm so obsessed with my nephew. He filled a space in my heart I didn't know was missing. He's already a hard-working little cowboy like his mom and dad. That was one of the many reasons I couldn't wait to get back to the ranch. I hate being away from him for too long.

I hear footsteps walking up to my trailer. My chest twists—for a moment I worry it might be Huck and he's found me. I peek out the tiny window on the front door and let out a breath when I see it's just Charli. She's back early and I flip the latch to unlock the door.

Fuck, I can't keep living on edge like this, and I know it's just a matter of time before I run into him at a rodeo now that I'm entering again.

Montana's pro rodeo circuit has thirty-two sanctioned rodeos. All of which I had planned on entering this summer. After my breakup with Huck, that didn't happen. I was so hung up on him and everything that happened between us. I couldn't bear the thought of seeing him.

The first rodeo I entered, someone mentioned he was there, and it anchored me where I stood—I froze up. I couldn't breathe and my chest was on fire. Charli helped me through a huge panic attack. She loaded up my horses, and we hauled ass in my truck and trailer as far away as we could get. She let me cry the entire drive and listen to depressing country songs about stupid cowboys who cheat and break hearts. It was actually quite therapeutic. We decided that night to camp out in the middle of nowhere. We drank two bottles of wine, cried, and sang our hearts out all night long. After that, I decided I would jackpot and work on the ranch the rest of the summer. I couldn't handle another panic attack like that, or a hangover for that matter. No more wine and crying over cowboys for me.

Unfortunately, I couldn't hide forever. I hadn't been winning shit at jackpots and I needed to enter a few pro rodeos to stay in good standings and keep my pro card. Then Charli convinced me to enter the Livingston Roundup this weekend. It's the biggest rodeo of the summer. But I knew the odds of running into Kenzington were growing by the hour.

I'm ready just in time, as Charli swings the door wide open. She does a little twirl and hair flip, showing off her outfit. She has on a denim miniskirt and a halter shirt that makes her boobs look amazing. Paired with her "going out" cowboy boots that give her height a little boost. They're squeaky clean and not covered in horse shit. The sunset makes her golden brown skin glisten.

I give her a whistle. "You look amazing. Have you been working out? Your quads are massive."

"I have a new trainer at Mountainrange Fitness. His name is Kody," she says, eyebrows dancing.

"Flavor of the month?" I ask with a smirk playing on my lips.

Her heart-shaped mouth curves into a wry smile. "You know I don't kiss and tell, Saxxon."

I tilt my head back and let out a howl. "Charli Kutler thinks she's sneaky now does she?" I deadpan.

She walks away laughing, her patience with me wearing thin.

Dash paws at my boot—his way of beginning me not to go. He tugs at my heart strings and I feel especially guilty after leaving him alone in the trailer for most of the day. I give him some extra food in his bowl to make up for it. I know I can always win him over with food. He's already forgotten all about me leaving.

Charli calls for me from outside the open door. "Sorrel, let's go, time to turn and burn, bitch." She pulls up her boobs so they look even perkier.

I shake my head. I am so not ready for this.

"Bye, Dash, love you."

He looks up at me with his half-blue, half-white

eyes that always make it look like he's sad. He's so damn cute. "I'm sorry, buddy. I wish I could stay. One more night and you'll be back at the ranch chasing cows and rolling in horse shit," I chuckle.

I step outside into the cool night air, and my skin prickles. Summer temperatures are dropping quickly, and it feels like fall is already rolling in. That happens early in Montana, but I get excited because even though our winters are frigid, it's one of my favorite times of the year.

Now that I'm outside, I look down at my outfit, feeling very underdressed. "Should I change?" I ask.

She looks me over, then rolls her eyes. "Sorrel, you could wear a damn paper sack and still look like a million bucks. Let's go."

I fumble with the keys and lock up the trailer.

"Finally, I thought you were gonna chicken out."

"I sure as hell thought about it," I mutter.

"Oh, come on. If Huck is there, I'll kick his ass."

She's so cocky considering Huck is double her height and mean as hell, but she might be meaner.

"Please, God, no. I don't want any trouble, Charli."

"I know, I know. All right then, we'll just ignore him and we'll dance our asses off to some Denton Reed."

"Oh, is that who's playing tonight? Do I know any of his songs?"

"You should! He's been playing at almost every rodeo this summer. Oh wait—that's right, you've been hiding out at the ranch all summer!" She teases.

I give her a playful shove.

Truth is, I have been hiding all summer. I'm just not ready to rehash everything and feel the trauma of it all again. It's better if I just pretend like it doesn't bother me, ignore my emotions, and move on.

She throws her arm over my shoulder and gives me a squeeze. After handing me the other beer she has, we clank them together and drink them as we walk to the arena entrance. I can already hear music playing and smell food coming from the food trucks set up outside the arena. I should eat something before drinking anymore tonight so I don't get a massive hangover before my drive home tomorrow.

We've almost finished our beers, and I get an optimistic feeling about tonight. Maybe I'll get lucky and Huck won't even be here. With any luck, he's already in his truck, halfway back to Fergus County, and he hasn't thought twice about me.

If only I could get him out of my mind.

"Sorrel, wake up!" Charli yells at me.

I spaced out thinking about last summer again. I've got to snap out of it.

"I'm awake. I'm ready. Let's get in there," I say with a nervous smile, and we stroll through the entrance.

3

SORREL

There are two opening artists before Denton Reed comes on. The arena is filling in, and I see a few familiar faces in the crowd. A few ladies I ran with today and some team ropers who are friends with Sutton's husband Ryder. I wave to the group of team ropers, and they all lift their beers and give me a nod back.

We put on a roping once a month in the summer at the ranch. It's always a fun time. The rigs roll in and the kids all jump out and take off to play in the dirt. When the roping is over, our ranch cook Jo makes a big feast for everyone buffet-style. It's a solid community, and we're lucky to be a part of it.

Charli walks us over to the group of barrel racers we ran with today. My stomach clenches when I see Emery Smith, Huck's other ex-girlfriend.

One of the few out of the group whom I actually like, Hailey, turns her attention to me.

"Nice run today, Sorrel. That was your young horse you ran?"

Emery glowers at me. I guess I won't be getting any compliments from her. Of course, she doesn't like me because she thinks I'm the reason Huck broke up with her. I had made sure they were broken up before we even started seeing each other; I know firsthand how these roughies can be.

I brush off Emery's dirty look and respond. "Yeah, it was. His name is Zip. I've ran him at a few local jackpots, but this was his first pro rodeo."

"Nice. I can tell he has drive; he's gonna be a good one," Hailey says.

"Thanks, I think—"

Emery cuts me off before I can finish. She brushes back her long black hair and squares her shoulders. "By the way, Sorrel, your horse looked a little lame when you left the arena. Might wanna get that checked."

Before I can respond she smirks and turns around, starting a new conversation.

Bitch.

I stick my tongue out at her from behind, and Charli bursts out laughing. It's childish, I know, but I don't care. I can't stand her. We're polar opposites. If anything, I would think she's more Huck's type than me. She's covered in tattoos and a little rough around the edges but still gorgeous.

Emery spins around, and I innocently shrug, pretending I don't know what everyone is laughing at. She scoffs and turns back to her conversation as if she's too good to give the rest of us the time of day. Someone really made her head way bigger than her ass, and I think I know who it was.

"C'mon, Sorrel, let's go get a drink at the bar," Charli says, grabbing my hand. I accidentally shoulder-check Emery while walking away.

Before she can do anything, a swarm of people swallows her up into the crowd. I turn around and see how pissed off she is. She's jumping up and down and trying to claw her way through them, but there are too many people. I smile and wave at her before we duck out of her sight. She's all bark and no bite.

We get in line for the bar, and Charli balls her fists and grinds her teeth. "I should fight her."

"Woah, easy now, killer," I jokingly calm her down like a spooked horse. "We're here to have fun, remember!"

That snaps her out of it and she shoots me a smirk. She's always down for a brawl. That was the reason she had to move away from Texas. Her mom was scared she was going to wind up putting someone in the hospital or end up there herself. I'm usually the levelheaded friend and nonconfrontational, but maybe this time I should turn her out to pasture and see what happens.

I let out a few deep breaths, trying to compose myself. The line for the bar moves quickly, and the tension in my shoulders eases when we make it to the front. There's every kind of liquor you could want, but our choice is always whiskey.

"What'll y'all have?" says the hot bartender with shaggy brown hair and a little scruff on his face.

Charli pulls her tits up and leans over the sticky bar. "Whiskey, straight up, two—make it a double, sugar." She winks, and he smiles, staring right where she wants him to.

"You got it, miss." He pours our drinks and scoots them across the bar, not taking his eyes off Charli. We take our money out to pay, but he pushes back the cash.

"This round is on me as long as you come back and see me again," he says, giving Charli a seductive smile.

"Well, that's mighty sweet of you. We'll be back real soon," she replies with her sweet, slow drawl.

He tips his head to her. "You better."

We take our drinks and look back to see him staring at her curvy glutes. "Gosh, I love using all my ASSets," she says, and we both combust into a fit of laughter.

I know anytime I'm with Charli my night will be full of belly laughs and lots of shit-talking.

"You be sure to give that man the tip he deserves," I tease.

"You know I will." She winks at me.

"Boots up, whiskey down!" we both say, clinking our plastic cups together so hard we lose a little of the liquid inside.

We came up with the catchphrase in college, and it's always been our thing ever since. I take a sip, and the whiskey burns as it slides down my throat, but the heat settles in my belly. For the first time all day, I feel myself letting go of all the uneasiness I'd been holding inside.

The rodeo announcer's voice blasts through the speakers. "Up next, who you've all been waiting for is the one and only Denton Reed!"

The arena is full now—we push past cowboys and cowgirls and a few fans you can tell came in from the city for the concert. It looks like it might get a little rowdy in here tonight. We approach the front-right corner of the stage. It's a smaller setup where you can get close to the artist. Concerts at rodeos are pretty small unless it's someone like Cody Johnson or Jason Aldean performing. I prefer the smaller concerts. It's exciting to see new artists who are still making a name for themselves. Sometimes they get here before the rodeo and will meet some of the athletes. It's pretty cool to see different aspects of the Western lifestyle.

Rodeo is a lot like putting on a concert. We're also performing for fans. If there were no fans, there wouldn't really be any point. That's what makes it rewarding—at least for me. For some, it may be the money or the attention, but that's not why I do it. It's a way of life, and knowing I might make a difference in one little cowgirl's day when she watches me turn those barrels means the world to me.

"Hey, girls, good to see you here tonight!" I turn to my right and see it's Len.

He's a tall, burly old cowboy who looks intimidating but is more like a big teddy bear. Len is a deputy for Dawson Country Sheriff's Office. He works off-duty at all the rodeos and sometimes at the local bar in town. They're still required to wear their uniform but it's a separate gig from the sheriff's office and a way for them to make some extra cash.

I started going to the Wagon Wheel when I was about twelve with dad while he had a few beers with his cowboy buddies. Bars are different in small towns, and they let us ranch kids in during the daytime. They like to have an off-duty deputy onsite during tourist season—it can get rowdy. While dad drank and caught up with his friends, we would play pool and drink Shirley Temples. Whenever Len was working, we would all whine when it was time for him to kick us out—usually when the bar got too busy or a tourist started acting up. He's always had my back since he started the gig working off-duty at pro rodeos and concerts. I feel safer knowing he's here if anything happens.

I don't know about other types of concerts, but country concerts can definitely get wild. Cowboys, liquor, and country music—you know there's always a scuffle waiting to turn up in the mix somewhere.

I give Len a big hug and he gives me a squeeze back. "Stay on your game tonight, Len. These cowboys just got paid, and I know where they're spending it." I gesture to the bar.

"I'm looking forward to throwing a few out. It's the highlight of my night." He huffs out a laugh.

I smile and turn my attention to the concert that's beginning to start. Who I assume is Denton Reed swaggers out onto the stage.

I think I have heard a few of his songs but never knew what he looked like. He sure as hell doesn't disappoint. I'm a damn sucker for a man in a striped pearl-snap shirt. He sits a red Solo cup on the stool next to the microphone stand, his guitar thrown over his shoulder.

Charli lets out a whistle sharp enough to blow my eardrums out."Well, hot damn!" she drawls. "I'd ride that man like a rank bronc, spurin' him and hoping he bucks *hard*."

I almost spit my whiskey out laughing. I love her dirty mouth and innuendos. She ain't wrong though. He's drop-dead gorgeous with chiseled cheekbones and blondish-brown hair that curls out of the bottom of his brown felt cowboy hat at the nape of his neck. He doesn't look bad from behind either, in just tight enough dark wash Wrangler blue jeans. Veins run over his flexed muscular arms as he strums his guitar.

Charli said his music had been getting more popular recently. He even has a few songs out on the radio. That's probably where I've heard him. I'm sure he'll get a fancy record deal and a big tour soon. That's how it usually goes—country folk are usually first to support these smaller artists, and know about them before anyone else. Take Zach Top for instance. I started listening to him years ago when he was just posting videos on Instagram. Now it isn't just cowboys and cowgirls that like his music. But once these musicians blow up we can't even afford to buy a concert ticket to see them anymore. Good for them, though, if they make it that big.

The rest of the band settle into their positions, two guitar players and a drummer. Denton Reed leans into the microphone. "Welcome, everyone, and thank y'all for being here tonight!" His voice is smooth and deep and it's even prettier when he starts singing his first song. It's a George Strait cover, so I know all the words. Charli and I sing along, holding each other, swaying back and forth, sipping our whiskey. She's right. I needed to get out. I've been cooped up at the ranch too long.

The past year since my breakup hasn't been easy —I've tried putting on a brave face. But it's getting to me, and if I don't face it soon, I never will. It's so easy to just hide out day after day in my cabin—my safe space. But that's not really living, is it?

A few more songs in and I turn to Charli, who's absolutely mesmerized by the man on the stage, actually all the men. Each one of them has a different style but they're all attractive in their own way. Charli's eyes are huge and bounce around to each of them. I smile at her and tap her shoulder.

"Hey, I'm gonna go get us another round. Do you wanna see your boyfriend, the bartender, or should you save our spots?"

"Nah, you go. I'll stay, there's plenty of eye candy right in front of me." She giggles, and I think the whiskey is getting to her.

I turn to head to the bar. I see there's one closer off to my left a few feet away from the stage so I pivot back and my face runs right smack into a big broad chest. I know that chest, the smell of that cologne.

The tattoos that swirl across those bulky arms. I look up, the whiskey in my stomach churning as I see my ex.

Huck fucking Kenzington.

"Thought I'd find you here, darlin'," he says with a dark chuckle.

He looks the same as when I saw him nearly a year ago. Huck Kenzington isn't gorgeous like the man on stage. He's dangerous and wild. The type of man I knew was going to break my heart at some point. He stands six feet four inches, with jet-black hair and a powerful jaw, pure muscle. He only ever wears the color black. Black button-up, black cowboy hat, and black caiman boots. He's one of the best bareback riders on the circuit, one of the few things his parents' money couldn't buy. Just raw talent. His dark, unreadable eyes make him intimidating and alluring at the same time to most women, and he knows it. He usually gets what and who he wants. Guess that's what had intrigued him about me—the chase.

I didn't give him the time of day at first. He had the words "BAD, DANGER, DO NOT TOUCH" practically written all over him. Little did I know in the long run I didn't stand a chance. He had a side to him I couldn't resist, a side he only showed me that most would never get the chance to see. I got caught in his snare. When I fell for it, I fell so fucking hard.

"What do you want, Kenzington?" I say, tone clipped. But I'm fucking shaking inside.

"Aw, c'mon Sor, don't be like that. I miss you, baby.'"

"Don't fucking call me that," I snap, turning my face away from his. Looking at him when he says my name disgusts me now.

I used to love the way he called me Sor. It would make me melt every time. But now anything he says puts an awful taste in my mouth. I need to get as far away from him as possible and something to wash it away.

Charli's attention is no longer on Denton Reed and his band. She comes running to my rescue, but it's too late. He's already grabbing me. Panic sinks in, and I freeze in place. Flashbacks flood my mind. There's nothing I can do—the feel of his touch paralyzes me.

"Let go of her, you piece of shit!" Charli screams.

"Oh, stop. You damned barrel racers are so dramatic." He shoves her back, not realizing how tiny she is. She goes flying.

That's when I snap out of it and wrench away from him.

"Don't you fucking touch her!"

"Fucking hell, Sorrel, quit causing a scene," he says as if I was the one who started it.

Len runs over, and I realize we are definitely causing a scene. Everyone's attention is on us, including Denton Reed. It's like the entire concert practically pauses as everyone in the crowd watches. Huck finally lets go once Len gets to us and gives him a don't-fucking-try-me look.

"Everything all right, girls?"

I narrow my eyes at Huck. "Yeah, everything's fine."

His eyebrows come together and his eyes go dark, a look that says this isn't over.

Len knows better than to leave him alone with us. He's very familiar with Kensington and his antics.

"Why don't you come on over backstage with me, girls?"

Huck is on our tails, following after us. Len turns around and put his hand up. "Just the girls, Kenzington."

Huck growls and squeezes his knuckles. Len puffs his chest out and crosses his arms. Is there about to be a showdown? Tension crackles in the air and it feels like we're in an old western. Who's going to draw first? Huck must have one good brain cell left because something in him tells him he won't be winning this duel. Or maybe it was the fact that his parents won't tolerate any more town gossip caused by him. The Kenzingtons are tired of their problem child. He's on his last leg with them before they cut him off completely.

I see the muscles in his jaw relax, and he gives us a mocking grin before turning on the heel of his boot. Huck walks back to his roughie buddies, who are all huddled around some buckle bunnies. They're all wearing plastic boots with their pants tucked in and crop tops that show off their thin stomachs. Huck throws his arm around one with bright red hair and a pointy face. She grabs his broad chest, practically salivating over him. I gag and feel the whiskey making its way up my throat. He turns back in my direction and looks at me before placing a kiss on the redhead's lips, trying to make me envious. His eyes are open the whole time he does it. Part of me feels bad for her. She has no clue that it's all for show. Charlie mouths "fuck off " and gives him the bird. She grabs my wrist, dragging me away.

We make our way to the side of the stage. I see Denton Reed's eyes drift over to us. I'm so incredibly embarrassed we just caused a scene during his show. I wish I could apologize; I'd be pissed if someone did something like that during one of my runs.

Now that we're so close to the stage, I'm able to make out his features. Not as rough as Kenzington but still just as sexy with a smile that could disintegrate your heart. He's about six foot three inches or taller if I could guess, and he's built on the leaner side but still firm and muscular. The way he lowers his eyes and looks at me like he's singing just to me has my stomach doing somersaults. I must be imagining it. I'm sure every girl who gets to be this close to the stage feels this way. For Christ's sake, he's a musician. I'm sure they're practically trained to do this. It's all the art of the act, I remind myself—he's a performer.

I'm still shaken up by everything that went down and I need a drink, bad. We're too far from the bar now, so Charli—the sweet-talkin' gal that she is—gets some guys hanging out backstage to give us their beers since they were double-fisting and had two fresh ones each. She's heaven sent, I swear it. I'm not sure what I did to deserve such a good friend.

I steady my breathing, easing my nerves. When I look up, Denton Reed's gaze is lingering in our direction again. I stare back, partly because we're at a concert and that's where I'm supposed to be looking. But also because I'm totally starstruck by him. I watch his alluring mouth as he tilts his head, lips grazing the microphone and eyes glancing in our direction every few seconds.

"Girl, I think he is looking at you," Charli says.

"No way, he's probably looking at you," I brush her off.

His shoulders are turned toward us instead of straight at the crowd and I'm beginning to think maybe she's right. I continue to stare at him, going along with whatever game he's playing at. My lips curl in holding back a smile. His are twitching in return, when he finally turns back toward his audience.

"Are y'all havin' fun tonight?"

The crowd cheers in response.

"We're gonna be taking a brief break here, and me and the boys will be back on in ten. Thanks, y'all!"

Denton Reed is walking over to where we're standing. My body buzzes, and I'm sure I have a deer in the headlights look on my face. Charli looks up at me and gives me a nudge with her elbow, and a shit-eating grin on her face.

4

SORREL

My stomach fills with butterflies, and my hands feel clammy. I don't know why the hell I'm so nervous. He's just a man. I'm surrounded by tons of them at the ranch, and it's not like he's that famous. Yet.

He approaches us both with a radiant smile. His short-sleeve pearl-snap shirt hugs his honed biceps. The snaps are unbuttoned just enough to see the smooth tan skin of his chest. The man with an incredible voice stops right in front of us.

"Hi, I'm Denton Reed," he says.

"We know who you are, obviously!" Charli blurts out.

The corner of Denton's mouth turns up. His eyes twinkle, a shade of deep emerald green. A little bit of scruff dusts his strong jawline. He looks like he might be in his early thirties.

"What are y'all's names?"

My cheeks flush, and my tongue feels thick in my

mouth. When I open it, nothing comes out. I've always been a little shy, but even when I met Huck, I didn't feel like this. Thank goodness for Charli—she answers for both of us.

"I'm Charli. This beautiful cowgirl who you've been making eyes at all night is my best friend Sorrel," she tells him.

I instantly change my mind about Charli answering for both of us. I think I might die of embarrassment now. We don't even know if it was me he was staring at.

He shakes her hand and then mine. His hands are rough and calloused. Not just a pretty boy with a pretty voice. Those are the hands of a working man–I know that better than anyone.

"Hi," is all I say.

Charli elbows me again, this time harder. I flinch away from her. "Ow! What the hell was that for?"

"You're being rude, Sorrel. Denton stopped his show to come and meet you. Didn't you, Mr. Reed?"

I look around, and the world comes back into focus. DJ B-star is in the back left corner of the stage in his booth. A Morgan Wallen and Shania Twain mix is playing through the loudspeakers. Cowboys and cowgirls are two-stepping in a circle on the dance floor in the middle of the arena grounds. There's no way he stopped the show to come meet me.

Denton Reed chuckles. It's a seductive deep laugh that makes me clench my legs together.

"Well, actually—I did, Miss Charli," he admits.

"Saw what happened down there with that husky boy—"

A snort escapes from Charli and I give her a pointed look.

He continues. "And something in me just wanted to make sure you're okay. This is my show after all, I want to make sure all my fans are having a good time."

"I'm not a fan," I tell him.

His eyebrows shoot up to the top of his forehead and a playful grin spreads across his face. "Well, I hope you will be after tonight."

I look over at Charli, a cheesy grin lighting up her face.

Fuck he's smooth.

"Well, y'all, I better get back to it," he says, then meets my eyes. "Hey, I don't have any plans after my show tonight and I think my band wants to go into town to the casino. I'm not the gambling type, so I was wondering if maybe I could buy you a drink after my show?"

Is he asking me—or Charli—or both of us? I can't tell.

Before I can get a word out, Charli says, "She would love to!"

He takes his cowboy hat off and rakes his hand through his wavy brownish-blonde hair.

"See you soon, cowgirl," he says with a wink as he puts his hat back on. When he's walking back to center stage, he shouts over his shoulder, "I'll meet you back behind the stage when the show is over. Remember now, have fun."

Charli waves goodbye quickly in big half circles over her head. "She'll be there!!" she shouts to him.

I narrow my eyes at her, hands on my hips and head tilted to the side. I hope she's ready for an earful. I peek over Charli's head as Denton takes center stage. He picks up the red Solo cup and I watch him bring it to his lips. His Adam's apple bobs up and down, and a little bit of whatever he's drinking slides down his chin and neck. Damn, why is that so hot? He flashes us one more smile before starting the concert again.

I lower my gaze back to Charli. No more distractions.

"What the fuck was that, Charli?"

"Don't pretend to be mad, Sorrel. I know you better than that. You didn't have the guts to say yes, so I did it for you."

"I am mad!" I shout at her. "I'm not interested in any men. I don't care that he's a country music star. He could be Sam Elliott in his younger years and I still wouldn't go for it."

She gives me an exacerbated look. "First off, Sam Elliott is so hot. Second, you've got to get back on the horse at some point, or you never will."

Something in me knows she's right. I can't even remember the last time I was alone with a handsome man.

"Ugh," I groan. The little devil on my shoulder says, *Why not have a little fun—dip your toes in the water?*

"Remember, honey, we ain't getting any younger, and if I recall, you have a birthday coming up…the big two-six."

I roll my eyes at that. She doesn't need to remind me.

A stupid, hopeless romantic side of me thought maybe Huck was the one. I never should have let my mind go there. But I did, and now I'm paying for it with a broken heart and trust issues. Settling down or marriage never crossed my mind much. I was always on the road or working on the ranch, and that kept me too busy to focus on a serious relationship. I'd had a few admirers in the past, but most couldn't even make it past Dad to get to me. Half of the guys in town would rather have a job at the ranch than date me and piss off my dad.

Two summers ago, Sutton got married. Seeing how happy she was that she found her person made me think maybe I want that too. Huck had been my date to her wedding. The way he looked at me while I stood next to my big sister while she got married melted my heart. But after what he did to me, it has long since frozen over again.

I sigh. "Fine, I'll meet with him, but only one drink and you're checking on my animals."

"Of course, babe, I'll even cuddle with Dashy and tuck him into his little bed."

We smile at each other, and she gives me a big hug. The concert is nearly over. Charli looks the band over one more time like she's trying to take a mental picture to save for later. Then she leaves to go check on my animals as promised. I walk toward the back of the stage. Len and the other deputies are standing in a circle, probably making a game plan for clearing the arena out. When Len sees me he pats one of the younger deputies on the shoulder then walks over to me.

"I heard from a little birdy Mr. Reed asked to have a drink with you."

Wow, gossip travels fast with these guys.

"He did, and wouldn't you know it, Charli is forcing me into it."

He snickers, shaking his head.

"Well, I asked around and heard he's actually a decent guy. You know I would tell you the truth. Your daddy wouldn't forgive me if I let you hang out with some wild, two-timing musician."

Nope that's just bareback riders, I think. I give him a tight smile in response.

"Have some fun, Sorrel. I'll be around if you need me."

"Thanks, Len, be safe out there tonight."

His job makes me nervous. I know how dangerous it is. Nowadays you never know what crazy person will show up at events to cause trouble.

I'm a barrel of nerves and I look around to see where I can get a drink. A little liquid courage might do me good. I find a private bar tucked in the corner. The bartender is slinging drinks left and right to all the people backstage. When the line clears, I walk over and give her my order.

"Can I get a shot of Pendleton please?"

Her brows come together and she scans me up and down. I stare back at her with a blank look on my face. She's pretty with brown glossy hair pulled into a slicked-back ponytail and brown almond-shaped eyes. Her big boobs are on display, sticking out the top of her tank top. Probably helps with tips, I assume.

"ID," she says flatly.

I dig my ID out of my pocket and hand it over to her. It doesn't offend me that she asks for it. I'm used to getting IDed most of the time when I order alcohol. Everyone has always told me I look young for my age. Baby face problems.

She throws it back to me across the bar and pours my shot—not even to the brim.

I scoff. "Thanks. How much is it?"

Her mouth falls open and her eyes light up. She stands up straighter, and a smile spreads across her face. I feel heat on the back of my neck. I turn my head to the right, and there he is.

"Whatever it is, put it on my tab," Denton says.

She clears her throat, her face going back to annoyance. "You don't have a tab. Your drinks are on the house."

He stuffs a hundred-dollar bill into her tip jar. "This should cover her shot then, right?" he asks her.

Tucking an invisible hair behind her ear, she purrs at him, "Uh, yeah, totally."

"Pour up two more of those shots, and this time to the brim," he says with a wink.

"We'll take two Ultra Lights too," I throw in. Hell,

if I have to watch her flirt with him, might as well get something out of it.

He looks down at me and smirks like he knows what I'm up to.

Turning his head back at the bartender, he asks her, "I'm sure the band will want a few before they head out. You don't mind sticking around, do you?"

Her back is facing us and she turns around, her cheeks a deep pink. In her hand are our two beers and a napkin. "Of course, thank you so much, Denton, and are your drinks." She puts the napkin in his hand, brushing her fingertips against his.

When I glance down at it, it says *Stephanie* and her phone number written underneath it. I choke on a laugh, and she narrows her eyes at me.

Looking down at the napkin, he bites back a laugh. "Thank you—uh…Stephanie."

God, I can't do this. I can't and won't compete with women who throw themselves at men like that. I throw back the half-full shot and the full one back-to-back.

"Cheers, to you too," he huffs a laugh, throwing his shot back.

We take our beers and leave the shot glasses on the bar. Denton gently places his hand on my elbow, steering me toward the stairs that exit the back of the stage.

"Where are we going?" I ask.

"I thought we could go somewhere a little quieter to enjoy our drinks, if that's all right with you."

When we get to the bottom of the stairs, A trash

can is off to the left. He crumples the napkin up and shoots it in like it's a basketball hoop.

I blink, honestly surprised. "You don't have to throw that away just because you're having drinks with me," I say to him.

His only response is raising an eyebrow while taking a swig of his beer.

"Just sayin' you might have better luck with her tonight than me."

I clearly have no filter tonight but it's the truth. I'm not the type to sleep around. No judgment to her or people that do, but I feel my emotions too deeply. I never liked the way it made me feel and I haven't been with anyone since my ex.

He swallows deep and licks his lips. I feel my body heat rising—flushed and a little embarrassed.

"She ain't the one I just bought a drink for," he finally responds.

I let out a short laugh. "The drinks were free, remember?"

We smile back at each other and I feel myself relaxing a bit. Letting the tension roll off my shoulders, I don't want to come across stuck-up. He doesn't deserve that. It's not like he knows my past or anything about me. We're just two people having drinks and then we'll probably never see each other again after tonight. I owe it to him to at least be kind. I owe myself to let loose and have a little fun.

He continues to lead the way to wherever he's taking us. I probably should actually find out before just walking off into the dark with this man I don't know. We're headed in the direction to the east parking lot. I parked my rig and horses in the west parking lot.

"Okay, you have to tell me where we're going now, mystery man," I quip and instantly cringe internally.

God, why is everything that comes out of my mouth so cheesy? It's like I forgot how to talk to a man.

"We're going—" He's cut off by a deep ragged voice that comes out from behind a rig.

"Where the fuck are you going with him, Sorrel?"

It's Huck. He must have been following us the entire time. Coming out from where he's hiding he stalks over to us. His face is dark and threatening, looking like he's about to snap someone's head off. Huck's eyes lock onto Denton's and his jaw clenches, knuckles white around a bottle of whiskey. I could smell the liquor on him earlier, and the bottle is nearly empty now. He's such a fucking asshole when he's drunk. Damned cowboys and not being able to hold their liquor.

Denton doesn't flinch. He casually throws his arm around my shoulder, keeping me close by his side.

"Didn't think you'd still be here, Kenzington," he says smoothly.

I can't lie and say I'm not impressed by the cool confidence that washes over him. Then it hits me that he said Huck's name. How in the hell does he know him? I look up at him, my brow furrowed.

He continues. "Thought you'd be off brooding

somewhere with your riggin' and a bottle, but I see you have the bottle part down."

Taunting Huck Kenzington is like playing with fire. My stomach turns into knots.

Huck turns abruptly, slamming the bottle down onto the back of someone's tailgate so hard it shatters into pieces. His hand begins dripping with blood. The spots are a deep red on the rust-colored dirt. He doesn't even look down at his injury, probably too drunk to feel it. He stumbles closer to us. I flinch but Denton holds steady.

Huck points at Denton, his voice low and rough. "Didn't think you'd be dumb enough to come near her."

I swallow my fear and walk toward him with my hands up like I'm trying to settle a spooked colt. "You're bleeding, Huck. Why don't you go get that cleaned up and call it a night?" I say, my voice pleading and soft.

Denton steps in front of me. "The only one not getting near her is you. As far as I can tell, Sorrel doesn't belong to anyone. Unless you branded her and I missed it."

Fuck, here we go. I can literally feel the heat rising between them.

Huck sneers. "You talk real big for someone who sings love songs and has never worked a hard day in his life."

Denton shoots right back. "And you act real tough for someone who got left in the dust, dead last today."

Huck must have had a shitty ride today that's

probably what initially set him off. When we were together, I had to walk on eggshells anytime he had a bad ride. I fucking hated it, not knowing if any little thing I said was going to cause an argument. Most of the time it did.

That last blow does it. Huck shoves Denton hard in the chest. I step back instinctively, heart pounding. Denton stumbles a step but comes back swinging. Not with a fist, but with his words. Maybe he isn't the fighting type.

"She made her choice, Huck. And it isn't you."

How does he know that?

Before either of us know it, Huck's fist is connecting with Denton's jaw. Huck is too fast for Denton to dodge, but he doesn't sway. He takes it on the chin, brushing it off as if it doesn't even faze him. Before Huck can swing again, a pair of thick arms come out of nowhere and lock around Huck from behind.

"All right, that's enough!" booms a voice as big as the man it belongs to.

Thank God, it's Len. I'd bet the ranch he's been tracking Huck, knowing he wouldn't leave me alone after finding me earlier.

He wrestles Huck back with ease, like he'd done it a dozen times before. Because he has.

"You know the rules, Kenzington," Len growls, as he hauls him through the parking lot. "Start a fight on my grounds, and you're done. You're trespassed from the property and I already called your buddy to come get you so don't think you're gonna run off now."

Huck thrashes once, eyes blazing, but Len doesn't so much as flinch.

Luke pulls up in his old Chevy truck and opens the door from the inside. "I'm so sorry, Sorrel, I should have kept a better eye on him."

"It's no one's fault but his," I respond, my voice hard. I'm so tired of everyone taking the fall for his piss-poor decisions. He needs to learn what accountability is, and I hope someone will teach him one day. Huck's friends have always been good to me. I'm not mad at them. But they sure do have questionable taste in friendships.

Len grabs Huck by the shoulders and throws him into the truck like a sack of grain. It's sort of funny to see him get thrown around by someone his own size.

Huck turns back just before the door slams. His glare meets mine, and I can see a storm of anger in his eyes. I have a feeling he won't be letting this go.

The door slams shut and they drive off. I let out a big exhale. Not realizing I had been holding my breath the entire time. I gulp down air, trying to catch my breath.

Denton rubs his jaw and lets out a low whistle. "That boy's got a hell of a punch," he mutters, flexing his jaw with a grin. "Not a lick of patience, though."

I look up at him, heart racing. "You okay?"

At least he's still cracking jokes, so maybe Huck hasn't totally ruined the night. But I was sure that would scare Denton off though. I'd imagine the last thing he wants is to hang out with a girl whose ex-boyfriend just punched him in the face.

He gives me a once-over and smiles softly. "I've had worse. You?"

"I've seen worse," I say, lips twitching. "But thanks for not punching him back."

He shrugs.

I'm still not over the way he took that punch. There's a slight red mark on his jaw and something in me wants to reach out and run my fingers along it. I tuck my hand into my pocket, resisting the urge.

"He wasn't worth spilling my beer. It ain't right not having anything to drink while getting to know a pretty cowgirl."

I can't believe he still wants to get to know me. What the hell is this guy thinking?

Shell shocked for a moment, I finally respond. "You still want that?"

Denton tips his hat, eyes gleaming. "Darlin', after all that? I think I've earned it."

And damn if he isn't right. He definitely earned it.

5

SORREL

An awkward beat of silence passes between us when we're now standing in front of a large bus. It's one of those big fancy ones that bands travel in and probably has a bunch of bunkbeds they all sleep in. There's no way in hell I'm going in there alone with him. If this guy thinks I'm going to crawl into his fucking bunk with him, he's about to find out just how wrong he is. I start to open my mouth and tell him exactly that, when he walks around to a small ladder on the side of the bus and pulls it down.

Gesturing up the ladder, he asks, "You comin'?"

A heat of embarrassment spreads across my chest, glad I didn't say anything. Putting my beer on my warm chest, I tuck my hair behind my ear. "I guess so," I say.

He takes my beer from my hand while I climb up first. I scoot over to the edge of the roof and sit, dangling my legs over the roof of the bus. I'm not scared of heights, but it sure is a long way down. He takes his place next to me, handing me back my beer. We sit there side by side, sipping our drinks and staring at the stars.

The sky is beautiful tonight, speckled with stars that look so big from up here, you can almost touch them. Every once in a while, I see a satellite flying through space, making its way across the world. As I watch another one float by, the nervousness I've been feeling around him all night finally begins to dissipate.

Denton eventually breaks the silence, and I appreciate him giving me time to process what just went down with Huck. I brace myself for the questions, thinking he's going to ask me what I ask myself—how could you be dumb enough to get involved with someone like Huck Kenzington. But that's not what comes out of his mouth.

He takes his cowboy hat off, sitting it down next to him. "So, I saw your run today, and you were amazing. That chestnut gelding you rode looked so damn powerful. The way he dug in around those barrels was smooth as hell."

He watched my run? That's right, he had made a comment to Huck about his ride too, so he must have watched the entire performance today. That must mean he already knew who I was then, before we even met tonight. And the fact that he noticed me on a plain chestnut gelding stands out to me. There're tons of gorgeous barrel racers with flashy horses that are way more memorable. I mean, I did probably win the average, but that won't be announced until after the last run tomorrow.

"Thank you," I say, raising an eyebrow. "I'm honestly surprised you watched the barrel racing. Most cowboys act like we're a bunch of princesses—"

"Always complaining about the ground?" he cuts in with a grin.

I laugh. "Exactly."

"Nah, I enjoy watching it." He puts his beer bottle between his legs and leans back on his hands. "My sister used to do 4-H, ran a few jackpots when we were kids. Nothing like what you pulled off, though. You make it look easy."

That catches me off guard, but in a good way. There's something different about him. Genuine. He isn't trying to impress me, and for once, I'm not just being sized up in tight jeans.

"Well, you were amazing tonight too. You've got an incredible voice, not that you don't already know that."

Denton gives me a toothy smile. "Ah, thanks. Truth is, I was a little nervous. This was one of my biggest shows so far."

I tilt my head, surprised. "Really? Because you looked like a total pro up there. If you're nervous now, I can't imagine what you'll be like when you're playing stadiums."

He chuckles, glancing down for a second before meeting my eyes again. "Yeah…that's the plan."

So… he's humble, handsome, and talented? Seriously, what the hell is he doing talking to me? But he is. And he isn't rushing it or putting on a show. He's just easy to talk to and a totally normal person like the rest of us. Maybe the fame just hasn't gone to his head yet.

Even in rodeo, it happens. People make it to the NFR, brand deals, you name it and then they think they're some big shot too good for everyone else. Fame has a way of changing people.

We talk for over an hour. I never move from my spot, but he climbs down once to get me a jacket when he notices I'm shivering. It's a Wrangler denim jacket. He lays it so gently over my shoulders. I can't help but bring my nose to my shoulder. It smells so good with notes of cedarwood and musk. Having his scent all over me stirs feelings inside of me that make me want to crawl out of my skin—in a good way.

Talking with him is like talking to an old friend. He tells me he's from Tennessee. No shock there. That's the capital of country music. I figure he probably started out somewhere near Nashville, maybe playing in smoky bars and county fairs before being discovered. I tell him I'm from Montana and grew up on a ranch called the Saxxon Ranch, but I don't go too deep into it. Just enough to keep the conversation flowing without giving too much away. We talk about rodeo, music, horses, travel, and everything in between. The conversation flows, and there's definitely a connection—whether it's just friendship or more, I'm not sure. But it doesn't matter because I'm not looking for more and I have enough friends.

I have to admit though, Charli was right. Getting

back on the horse feels good—it's as if I never stopped riding, muscle memory takes over. Just talking to a man, no pressure, no expectations. It's not a date; it isn't anything too intimate. Hell, it isn't even reality. It's just a moment. A soft, unexpected pause in the middle of a life that rarely slows down. There's that feeling though between us, the kind you feel in your chest but try to ignore in your head. This time I will ignore it because let's be real, our worlds don't exactly fit.

I spend a lot of time on the road for rodeo, and when I'm not chasing barrels, I'm at the ranch. Between managing the guests and helping out with ranch work, there's not much time in between for anything else. My family is everything to me, and it takes a special kind of person to understand my lifestyle, just as I'm sure the same would be for him. He's on a tour bus half the year, playing in different cities every weekend, chasing a dream that doesn't leave much room for staying in one place.

Whatever this little spark is, I have to face what it really is—a nice conversation on a beautiful night—between two people who are attracted to each other but know it will never be anything more than this. But damn…it was nice while it lasted.

My gaze lowers to his mouth as he speaks to me. He has a beautiful mouth. Lips that sure as hell looked kissable. I'm sure he is good at it too. I push that thought out of my head—time to get out of here before I do something I'll regret.

I sit up straight. "Thank you for the drink,

Denton. It was nice getting to know you a little. I had a good time tonight." I stand up, make my way toward the ladder, and climb down before he can try to convince me to stay.

"Wait, Sorrel—"

There it is. Fuck. I gotta get out of here.

He chases after me, shimmying down the ladder himself. His boot catches on the metal bar and he nearly slips. We both gasp and then he starts laughing.

"I'm fine. Just hold on a minute please before I kill myself on this damned thing."

"Okay, I'll wait," I say. I'm forced to stay put, standing there patiently so he can safely make it down. I'd feel terrible if he got hurt chasing after me.

He lets out a breath of air once he's down on solid ground. I shrug off his jacket and hold it out to him. He takes it from me and rakes his hand through his hair.

"Can I walk you back to where you're staying?" he asks.

"Oh, uh…sure. My rig's parked on the west side of the lot."

We walk in silence, the night air cool against my cheeks. It's quiet now except for the crunch of gravel beneath our boots. I keep my head on a swivel, silently praying we won't run into any more trouble. When we reach my trailer, a few soft whinnies greet us from the pens nearby. I smile at our greeting.

Pointing to my rig, I say, "This is it. Thanks for walking me back."

"Of course, it's my pleasure," he says, tipping his cowboy hat so proper I let out a quiet chuff.

He hesitates for a moment, then scratches the back of his neck. "So, uh…do you think we could maybe exchange numbers? Just in case I ever have more urgent questions about barrel racing or… something?"

He's joking—kind of. I pinch my lips together. But reality is already creeping back in. I have an itch in the back of my mind I can't scratch. Something's off… That's when the memory hits me like a freight train.

"How do you and Huck know each other?" I blurt out, brows knitting together.

The look on his face tells me that there's something he's hiding.

He pinches the bridge of his nose and looks down at his boots. "We rodeoed together in college—he's always been an asshole. I never liked the guy." He pauses, but I sense there's more coming. "I have to be honest with you, Sorrel. I was back behind the chutes during the bareback riding with a couple of buddies I haven't seen in a while. I overheard him talking about you. He knew you were here and was talking about finding you after your run."

"So, you already knew my name? It wasn't my raw talent and sorta good looks that caught your eye?" I tease, knowing I had already figured that out earlier. And I obviously knew Huck would have known I was here. He always watches the barrel racing so I'm not surprised he planned on trying to find me.

He laughs and shakes his head. "Well, yes and no—truthfully, when you came out of the alleyway and I heard the announcer say your name, I recognized it. I saw your picture on the big screen and how beautiful you were—I mean are. I can't lie, a thought crossed my mind—I need to meet that girl—and well, here we are."

"Well, I guess it's your lucky night, Denton Reed. You can thank Charli too. If it wasn't for her, I'd be home by now."

"Really? Shoot, then I better start counting my lucky stars. Maybe I'm lucky enough to get that phone number from you then?" He smiles big, a small dimple forming on his left cheek.

It's so cute, I bite the inside of my cheek and look away. But the fact that he and Huck know each other makes me question everything. They obviously have some sort of history. Maybe this is some kind of competition over girls that's been an ongoing thing. I want to give him the benefit of the doubt, but I'm not sure I can. The hesitation I'm feeling lingers like a dark cloud over my head. I have to go with what my gut is telling me.

"Honestly, I had a great time with you tonight. But we live two wildly different lives, and I'm just not in the right place right now to explore anything with anyone—uh, not that I'm—uh, assuming you want to… I know you were just asking for my phone number but my answer is no." I meet his eyes, hoping he can see I mean it kindly.

He clutches his chest and keels over. "Ouch, you barrel racers are ruthless."

I laugh nervously and shrug. "I'm sorry."

Barrel racers are kinda ruthless. We don't let much come between us and our goals. I know a lot of girls who won't even date, they're so focused on making it to the NFR.

The corners of his eyes crinkle, and he looks a little sad, but he doesn't push, doesn't charm his way around it. I wonder if he's ever faced rejection. It doesn't seem like it.

"Of course," he says with a small nod. "I get it completely. Have a good night, Sorrel."

And just like that, he turns on the heel of his boot and walks off into the dark. I stand there for a second, blinking, a little shocked he didn't try harder. But then again...why would he?

A guy like Denton Reed can probably get any girl's number without even asking. Even if he does seem like a nice guy, I'm sure he gets around like the rest of them.

Sighing, I go into my trailer and start getting ready for bed. Charli has my pajamas laid out for me. She picked a brown two-piece set with pink hearts on the shorts and a top that reads *heartbreaker*.

Yeah, right, I think.

I climb up into my bed that's at the nose of the trailer and lift Dash in with me. I put a new mattress in recently and it's still breaking in—a little stiff. Dash curls up under his blanket next to me already fast asleep. But sleep doesn't come easy for me. I toss and turn, restless and annoyed with myself. Replaying the night repeatedly in my mind. Why can't I stop thinking about him? It's not like I care. I didn't even want to have that drink with him.

Finally, exhaustion wins, and I drift off into a light, uneasy sleep. Saying no to giving Denton my phone number replays in my head all night. It's like an old DVD player that restarts the movie every time it's finished. Fall asleep—wake up—and there it is playing again, blaring loud.

At 6:00 a.m. sharp, I'm jolted awake by the sound of a snort and a pair of wide, curious eyes staring at me. A silly side of me thought maybe I would wake to a knock on my trailer door and maybe that person would be a handsome cowboy with a warm baritone. Even better with a coffee in his hand, but that never happens. I need to quit fantasizing about this guy. I think all those romance novels I read over the summer are getting to me. "Let's head home, Dashywoo," I say as we get out of bed, ready for the trek back to the ranch. If you don't have ten different nicknames for your dog do you really even love them?

6

DENTON

I wake up still thinking about Sorrel Saxxon. She's all beauty and grit, wrapped up in something I can't quite put my finger on. It wasn't just her long white hair or her sweet lips and piercing eyes. I felt drawn to her, and not just because she turned me down. Hell, I hadn't been turned down by a woman in—I can't even remember the last time if I'm being honest. While it stung a little, it also felt real. It's like it brought me back to reality.

Not to sound cocky, but it kind of comes with the lifestyle. Women practically throw themselves at me and my band members. It's part of the package when you're living life on the road in the music industry.

The thing is, women throwing themselves at me never really interested me. I, of course, appreciate beautiful women, but that's not why I wanted to become a musician. I struggled with my emotions when I was younger, and music became an outlet for me. It made me feel alive, and it was the best way I could express myself. I started getting serious about it in college.

After high school, I got accepted to Texas A&M. I was studying to get a bachelor of science in architecture and doing college rodeo. I would bring my guitar to all the rodeos, and everyone would gather around while I played and sang songs I had written. At some point I realized I was better at singing and playing a guitar than rodeo and schoolwork. I dropped out my junior year and moved to Nashville to see if I could make something out of it all.

Well, lo and behold, I was getting more and more gigs and everything was taking off. I'd been laser-focused on my career for so long, so dating was the last thing on my mind. I'd had a few relationships here and there, but nothing serious.

Most weekends, I was grinding—playing every dive bar and back porch stage in Nashville, hoping someone from a label would notice me. But that's not how it went. I didn't get discovered; I built it. I'd post every show we played at on our social media platform. It started with a few hundred views to a few thousand, and from there, it snowballed. Bigger shows. Bigger crowds. Every weekend, another stage. We hired our agent Jake to help us manage it all. Then we got this gig from a buddy of mine at all these rodeos this summer. I thought why the hell not? It's probably the most fun I've had in a while performing, getting the best of both worlds. People online are eating this shit up. They love rodeo and country music.

It fires me up before every show getting to go back

behind the chutes and hangout with all the roughies like old times. When I overheard Huck Kenzington talking about a barrel racer named Sorrel Saxxon, I didn't think much of it—other than he should keep his damn mouth shut and quit bragging about being with women. But then during the barrel racing, her picture was up there on the big screen. She had the most beautiful turquoise eyes I'd ever seen, and her smile—God her smile—it stretched so wide you could see most of her perfect top teeth. It was a beautiful smile that really stood out. Try as I might, I just can't get Sorrel out of my mind.

My daydreaming is interrupted when I hear the door to the bus open. It's Johnny, our lead guitarist, he's humming a tune, a smile plastered to his scruffy face. "You up, Denton?"

"Yep, I'm right here," I say over my shoulder, pouring myself a cup of coffee and trying to shake off the haze from the night before.

Johnny steps into the kitchenette, grinning like he already has a story to tell. "So?" he says. "How'd it go with that gal? You get lucky?"

I shake my head and take a long swig of coffee. It's strong, hot, and exactly what I need.

"She was a nice girl. We just talked is all."

"Lame," he says, grabbing himself a mug. "I'm tellin' you, man. You gotta get out there. You're almost thirty. The older you get, the harder it is to find one that doesn't have kids, a divorce, or both."

He's not wrong, but those aren't deal-breakers for me.

"I ain't worried 'bout it. When the right one comes along, I'll know. You don't need to worry about my dating life anyhow." Between him and the gossip columns on the internet, everyone is way too concerned with my dating life.

"How was that casino? You boys walk away with some cash?"

He looks like a hot mess in a way only a true road dog can pull off. His hair is wild and tangled, like he'd slept in a hayfield, pearl-snap shirt half-open and wrinkled. He still has on his Wranglers from last night, faded and creased, boots scuffed and tucked in sloppy.

"Parker and I ran into a pack of buckle bunnies after the show. We figured we'd have more fortune with them than the casino," he says with a devilish grin. "Man, we tore it up. And by tore it up, I mean we tried to keep up without embarrassing ourselves." He winks and takes a long pull from his coffee.

"Well, I'm glad you boys are enjoying yourselves. You deserve it. We've put in the work to get here, and I appreciate the hell outta y'all."

Johnny raises his mug in a mock salute. "Yeah, well, you deserve to have some fun too, Denton. Can't be all work and no play. Plus, how are you gonna get inspiration for new songs if you don't actually live it?"

He's right. I haven't let myself have much fun in a long time. I've been too focused on making it, but what was the point of it all if I wasn't happy? But damn it, I did deserve to enjoy it. I knew I was approaching burnout and I needed to make a change.

I slam my cup down, coffee spilling onto the counter. "Ya know, you're fucking right, Johnny," I say, straightening up. I have an idea—it's probably a bad idea—but still a grin tugs at my lips. "I think it's about time I start having a little fun. And I know exactly how to do it."

Johnny raises a brow, eyes lighting up. "Oh yeah, Dent? Well, what the hell! You know I'm always down for a good time. What've you got in mind?"

Last night I tossed and turned in my bunk. I couldn't get Sorrel off my mind. I tried to distract myself by scrolling on my phone, but I ended up on the internet typing into Google "Saxxon Ranch". Sorrel didn't tell me much about it, but my curiosity got the best of me. The screen loaded, and I clicked on the website for the ranch. The first picture was of a breathtaking mountain range, rivers running through a valley, and little pink flowers in bloom. Montana sure is beautiful. I was about to click on the drop-down to where it said "photos" but something caught my eye—guest ranch. My finger hovered. *Click.*

"That gal I hung out with last night. Her family owns a ranch."

"Okay and…?"

I'm not sure why I feel embarrassed to tell him this.

"Well, after she said no to giving me her number—"

"Wait, what? She said no? Something must be wrong with this girl."

I shake my head. "Anyways, I looked up the ranch and it turns out they've got a guesthouse for rent. I figured you, me, and the boys could head up there, get a little R&R. Says it comes with three home-cooked meals a day, actual ranch life experience, and there's a little town nearby with a bar that looks like a proper hole in the wall. Thought we might raise some hell, clear our heads for a bit."

He tilts his head back and lets out a loud laugh. "I get it. You dig the chase. Well, fuck yeah, I'm in! Book it! I'll round up the guys and we'll hit the road."

"Seriously?"

"Hell yeah, this is gonna be awesome! I can't wait to see her face when we show up."

Johnny disappears out the door, already fired up before I can give him all the details. We have one more show tonight a few towns over, so we won't be able to go to the ranch until tomorrow.

I grab my phone off the counter. Pulling the ranch website back up, I click on the phone number listed at the bottom of the page. My stomach feels queasy—partly from the alcohol last night, caffeine this morning, and no food. And I'm not sure who will be on the other line.

Ring, ring, ring.

"This is Clint. What can I do for ya?" a deep and raspy male voice says.

"Yeah, uh, I wanted to inquire about renting out your guesthouse. Is it available?"

"Yeah, it's available," Clint says in a short, clipped tone.

"Okay…we could get there as soon as tomorrow morning. Can we get it for a week?"

"Yep, that'll work. See you tomorrow."

Click.

"Hello, are you there?" I ask into the phone. Well, all righty then. I guess it's as simple as that.

A nervous twist hits low in my stomach. The thought of seeing Sorrel again with that long blonde hair, and that fire behind her eyes. It damn near knocks the breath out of me. Yeah...I have it bad already.

The rest of the band comes barreling into the trailer along with Johnny. Where the hell did they all sleep last night? The only one who rolls out of their bunk is Grady, our bass player.

Rubbing the sleep out of his eyes, he asks, "What's going on?"

"We're going to a dude ranch, yeehaw!" Johnny says, jumping up and down, twirling an invisible rope in the air.

"I rented us a guesthouse on a ranch for a week. It's about time we had a vacation—now if you'd rather go home, I understand. Next concert is in two weeks, so it's up to y'all."

"We're in!" they all announce at once, except for Grady.

We all look at him.

He groans. "Uh, fine, I'm in."

Johnny grabs him by the shoulders and gives him a pat on the back. "All right, that's the spirit, buddy!"

We pack up and get everything squared away.

One more show and I can finally relax. I long to be on the back of a horse, with the warmth of the sun across my back and, hopefully, a pretty cowgirl to look at.

We have almost a two-hour drive to Billings for tonight's show. The Saxxon Ranch is just south of Billings in the Pryor Mountains.

I sit up front next to Ray. He drives the bus for us and helps set up and take down the set at every concert. We did everything ourselves before, but we hired him this summer and it's been a hell of a lot easier. We damn sure appreciate him. I type in the address from the website for Saxxon Ranch. About three hours from tonight's venue, it reads. With stops, it will probably be about four, so we'll get a couple hours of sleep after the show and make it there by morning.

7

SORREL

I make it back to the ranch just before sunset. As I crest the mountain, the valley opens up below me, and there it is—our gate—standing tall and proud. The wooden beam across the top, that's stood the test of time—Saxxon Ranch. Bold and familiar, just as it has been since I was a kid.

I slow the truck and take it all in. The valley is beautiful this time of year, little pink wildflowers scattered like confetti across the grass, which is so green it almost doesn't look real.

The setting sun lights the sky on fire, painting everything in shades of orange and red that make the land glow. God, I love it here.

As I pull into the gate, the ranch dogs come tearing down the drive to greet me.

"Hey, boys, we're home," I call out through the open window.

Sally Jo, my dad's feisty little blue heeler, barks like

she's been waiting for this all day. The two Great Pyrenees, Ranger and Rooster, let out low, rolling howls as they prance over, tails wagging. Dash, who's been whining from the front seat for the last ten miles, loses his mind with excitement. I open the door, and he bolts out, ears flopping, racing to catch up with the others as they take off toward the main house. I smile, watching them disappear into the distance, my heart already lighter. It's good to be home.

I drive up the road, waving at a few ranch hands working colts in the arena. Today is Sunday, so most of the crew has the day off if they want, but a handful usually stay back to keep things running. The young ones, though, always head into town to the local honkytonk to throw back a few beers and tie one on.

I pull my truck and trailer in front of the barn so I can unload the horses. Our barn is beautiful and rustic. We fixed the roof this spring and it was painted red. The rest of the barn is natural wood; it's my favorite building on the ranch. A fixture that has charm, character, and a story to tell.

But now when I look at the barn, I don't get that same warm feeling that I used to. All I see is him and the night I wish never happened. Most of the time I can't bring myself to go in. I've been asking the ranch hands to put my horses up or take them out for me. They probably think I'm a spoiled, lazy brat. But they can think what they want. I'm just worried Sutton is going to say something about it soon.

The barn itself holds twenty stalls and has a large tack room. Next to the tack room is Dad's office, always cluttered, papers everywhere. I'd tried to organize it a few times in the past, but every time he caught me, he'd just growl and say that he works better in chaos. So, I let it go.

"Hey, Dad! You in there?" I call into the open barn.

"Yeah, Sorrel! That you?" His voice carries from the breezeway.

"It's me, your favorite daughter!" I singsong.

I hear his raspy laugh in response.

I unload Duke from the trailer and tie him to the hitching post out front. Peeking my head into the barn, I see Dad is tending to his old horse, Cowboy, cleaning out his feet in the crossties. He drops his foot and stands while rubbing his lower back.

"How was the rodeo, sweet pea?"

"It was good! I finally won a check," I yell out to him, trying to sound proud.

"All right, good job, baby! I've got some news too. Come on in here, would ya?"

I slowly make my way into the barn, positioning myself so my back is to the haystack.

"Someone booked the guest ranch house. We're gonna be real busy for the next few weeks. I was hoping you could help out while they're here."

"Yeah, of course. Any idea who it is? What they're expecting?"

"Not sure. You can reach out if you want—info's in my office—you know I'm bad at this stuff. They want to move some cattle and pretend to be real cowboys. You know, that kind of thing." He chuckles.

Building and renting out the guesthouse had been my idea to help bring in some extra cash flow. Sutton hated it, said we weren't a dude ranch, but it made a difference financially, so it was worth it. We've had some interesting guests. All kinds of people from doctors to actors and even regular old horse people who know how to ride but want to experience what a working ranch is like.

"All right, sounds good. I'll make sure the guesthouse is ready for them first thing in the morning," I say.

"Lucy already got to it, but I appreciate ya, darlin'," he says with a smile, then pulls me in for a hug and kisses my forehead.

Lucy is our housekeeper. She's been a blessing I didn't know we needed until we had her. With three cabins and two bunkhouses, it's a lot to keep up with, especially when you live with cowboys. Their definition of clean is an entirely different one than mine.

After walking into Dad's office, I rummage around through piles of papers scattered across his desk. I find one that has tomorrow's date written on it and reads: *guest ranch rented for tomorrow morning.*

Well, that's real descriptive… not. I swear his office is about as scrambled as my brain. So we have no information for the guests tomorrow. Great. This is exactly why I don't like being away from the ranch for too long.

A squeal from a little voice outside the barn pulls me from my rambling thoughts. "Auntie Sorieeee!"

It's Trotter. He's standing with Ryder by my truck looking all around for me.

I beam, seeing how excited he is that I'm home.

"Trot trot!" I call for him.

He comes running and jumps into my open arms.

"I missed you, Auntie Sorie," he says.

He nuzzles his head into the crook of my neck and it tickles. I laugh. I love how cuddly he's become at this age. He's almost three now and growing like a bean sprout. I pull him away from me so I can get a good look at him. His bright blue eyes and dimples melt my heart. He looks a lot like his dad with olive-colored skin and similar features, but he got his dirty blonde hair and blue eyes from Sutton.

"I missed you too Trotty. Did you take care of all the animals while I was gone?"

He looks at Ryder with confusion on his face.

"We sure did. Remember Trotter, we doctored the calves yesterday," Ryder says.

"Yeah!" he exclaims, clapping his hands.

I set him down on the ground and he takes off in a sprint toward Duke. I untie him and hand Trotter the lead rope. It's absolutely adorable how Duke just follows him like a puppy dog. He's the best horse. I've had him since he was a colt. He looks just like his mama, a stocky bay roan with a black mane and tail. Duke's thirteen now, but you would never know it. He's full of spunk and still my best barrel horse.

"You coming to dinner tonight?" Ryder asks.

I've missed Jo's cooking so much, and I'm craving a home-cooked meal after being on the road. Jo cooks three meals a day during the week. On Sundays, she only makes dinner, and everyone eats in the main house. Sunday dinner is an all-out affair and usually lasts several hours. I have so much to do before the guests get here. If I go, I'll never get it done.

"Actually, I'm gonna go check on the guesthouse before tomorrow morning and unpack, so I'll probably just eat at my place tonight."

"Sounds good. See ya in the mornin' then," Ryder says, tipping his head.

"See ya!" I say.

He walks away to get Trotter, who's wandered into Dad's office and has started making even more of a mess.

I hurry to finish unloading everything from the weekend. The worst part about being on the road is settling back into one place.

I leave Duke and Zip tied to the hitching post, knowing dad will put them up for me. Lastly I unhitch my trailer and then drive up to my cabin. Dad lives in the main house, and my cabin is just next door to his. It's a modest two-bedroom, two-bath cabin, perfect for just me. Sutton, Ryder, and Trotter live in the house farthest from Dad's. It has three bedrooms and two baths but desperately needs to be updated. They need more space now since their family has grown, and renovations will be starting soon. Near the arena and barn stand the guest ranch house, a five-bedroom, three-bath cabin, the newest on the ranch. We built it specifically for renting out, and it has already paid for itself. Behind the barn are the bunkhouses where the ranch hands live. There's two bunkhouses and we have about five cowboys currently living between the two of them. They all range in age and some are part-time and a few full-timers that have been working here since I was a kid. Honestly, we probably have too many hands working for us. Dad has a big heart and isn't willing to let anyone go. But now that we have extra income from the guest house, our ranch has been profitable year after year.

"Ah, home at last," I sigh as I step inside my cabin. Dash comes running in behind me, hopping right into his plush bed by the fireplace. My place isn't big by any stretch, but it's cozy, and perfect for me and my little dog. I'm on the road so much in the summer. I don't need a big ol' house. Maybe it'd be different if I had someone to share it with, but at this rate, I'm not holding my breath.

Dad must have started a fire for me when he knew I was close to home. That man gets sweeter and sweeter in his old age. I stoke the fire until the flames crackle and dance, then plop down on my plush light brown couch, curling up into a faux fur throw. Exhaustion hits me like a ton of bricks after the unsettling weekend.

I'm still questioning whether not giving Denton my phone number was the right decision. Am I crazy to think we had a genuine connection…or was it all for show?

It's probably all in my head. I mean hell, he's a

musician who could have any woman he wants. I need to get a grip.

My stomach rumbles. Damn, I haven't eaten much all day. I crack open the fridge to find not much of anything. I'll have to run into town tomorrow for groceries and snacks for the guesthouse. While I'm there I'll stock my fridge for times like this. For now, I settle for some lunch meat that is just barely still good and a handful of chips. Dash is begging at my feet, eyes glued to the lunch meat.

"You got food in your bowl," I grumble, but his begging is relentless. I give in and break off half a slice of turkey. "That's all you get buddy."

I turn my attention to the couch where I can just barely make out a faint buzzing noise.

Buzz, buzz, buzz.

There it is again. My phone must have fallen out of my pocket and escaped into the couch cushion. I pad over to the couch and tilt my head listening for the buzzing noise. I dig behind the cushion. "Got ya!" I say and bring the screen to my face. My phone is still going off and I have three missed calls and two text messages from Charli. My brain feels fried, and I don't have the energy to get into everything tonight, so I send her a text.

SORREL:

I'm home and will call in the morning.

CHARLI:

What the hell??? Call me now! I can't wait another minute. I need the TEA ASAP.

She's definitely going to be annoyed when I don't respond tonight, but she'll get over it once I give her all the juicy details.

—

I wake up groggy, already dreading the busy day ahead. After rolling out of bed, I flip on the fancy espresso machine my mom got me for Christmas last year. Caffeine is an absolute necessity. One honey latte coming up. The double shot of espresso drizzles into local honey I bought at a farmers market in town a few weeks ago. I grab my favorite dachshund mug from inside the cabinet, pouring in the espresso and then milk. Taking a sip, I savor the sweet honey mixed with the bold espresso and whole milk. It's like summer in a cup.

I decide on my usual jeans and a T-shirt and grab my sherpa pullover from the chair in the corner where my laundry pile lives. Lucy was adamant I let her help me with it, but I told her not to bother. It's something I'll have to tackle one of these days, but there's a system to my madness.

I pull the sweatshirt over my head, I simultaneously knock over the stack of books next to the laundry. I yelp, stubbing my toe on a romance novel. I've been meaning to read that one. I pad over to the couch, where I slipped my boots off last night. I hop up and down, slipping on one boot, then the other. I head out the door with a slam.

"Shit, Dash." I turn back around and open the door. My sidekick comes darting out, ready to go run errands.

My Dodge Cummins pickup fires up, and I drive into town, about a forty-five minute drive to the nearest grocery store. On the radio, Denton Reed's new song "Wild" comes on. It's about a young, wild guy who never grew up, while his girlfriend did. The guy is still deep in the bar scene, and the song goes on about how he should have given her a ring and a house full of kids. I think that song tells me everything I need to know.

Just as I'm pulling into the Shop and Stop parking lot, Charli's name lights up on my dashboard screen. Fuck, I forgot to call her back this morning. I press the green phone button to answer.

"Sorrel Saxxon, this is your best friend in the whole world, making sure you're still alive." Charli's voice crackles through the speaker.

"Yes, I'm still alive, no need to worry! I was just exhausted when I got back to the ranch. We have a decent-sized group coming to stay this week, so I'm in town for supplies."

"Oh, well, okay, I guess that's a reasonable excuse for not filling me in on how the night went, but next time you don't let me know you made it home safe, I'm driving my ass up there just to give yours a beatin'."

I laugh. "Yes, ma'am, I won't let it happen again," I say, trying for a stern tone.

"I'm holding you to that, Sorrel. Anyway, give me all the details."

I go over everything that happened, filling her in on Huck punching Denton and then Len kicking Huck out. She's eating it up. I can hear her wicked grin through the phone. When I tell her I refused to give him my phone number, she about blows a gasket.

"What the fuck, you didn't give him your number? What on earth is wrong with you, Sorrel?"

"Nothing, I'm just not interested."

"Yeah right, I know you and he is right up your alley!" Charli cries out.

She isn't wrong and that's the problem. Obviously, my choice in men is questionable. I'm trying to make better choices.

"I'm just not ready Charli, I need to work through my past. I still haven't compartmentalized it all. Anyhow, I don't think dating a musician is any smarter than dating a cowboy. I learned my lesson."

"I'm rolling my eyes at you right now."

"Oh stop. Listen, I just got to the Shop and Stop. Can we talk about this later?"

"Anyone interesting staying this time? Oh, I hope it's Kevin Costner! We could show him the real Yellow Stone experience," she teases.

Tilting my head back, I laugh. "Not sure. Dad didn't write any names. He's killing me, Charli."

"Well, good luck! Let's get together soon. Love you!"

"Love you too."

I press end and let out a raspberry, glad she didn't push me further. I roll the windows down for Dash. It's plenty cool enough out for him to wait in the truck while I shop.

It takes me nearly an hour to hunt down everything on the list. Usually, Jo handles the grocery shopping for the ranch, but I sent her a text last night offering to pick up groceries since I was going into town. I try to help out wherever I can but I'm regretting it now as this list seems never-ending.

Next I stop to get fuel, and some feed to keep stocked in my trailer. It's now almost ten o'clock in the morning. The guests are supposed to check in at some point this morning but since Dad didn't get the exact time they would be arriving. It could be any minute now. He isn't out ranching though, so he'll be there to check them in. Still, I'm eager to get back and get to work.

As I'm driving through town, I spot the mobile coffee truck parked on the side of the road. The rustic roast has the best damn coffee—and it's the only coffee shop—in town. All right, one more latte and then I'll get out of here.

I walk up to the window and place my order.

"Hey, Jessie! Can I get a cookie-butter latte please?" I went to high school with Jessie. She's a nice gal and her coffee truck has been doing great this summer.

"You got it, girl!" she says as she starts to brew the espresso.

"Omg, you'll never get this—I had a group of the hottest guys stop at my truck today and they left a fifty-dollar tip. I could tell they were out-of-towners, way too good looking to be from here."

"Wow, that's awesome! I bet that made your day!" I say, giving her a warm smile.

"Hell yeah, it did! We don't get that too often around here and it's my biggest tip I've ever gotten."

"Well, how about I'll match it and make your day twice as sweet." I say, stuffing cash in her tip jar.

"OMG, Sorrel, you're the best. Tell your family I said hi!"

"Will do. Have a good one, Jessie," I tell her as I leave and take a sip of the latte she made me. Fuck that's so good. I should get the recipe. But I don't have time. I've got to haul ass out of town and get back to the ranch.

Just as I pass the local bar, I spot a black Dodge dually with a stock trailer hauling three horses. It's Kenzington's rig. That POS has no business being at the bar in the morning with horses loaded in his trailer. What the hell is he doing in Lexington anyway? Maybe picking up horses from a nearby ranch? Either way, I don't like seeing him in my town, at the bar I usually go to with my friends. I flip him off as I drive by. Not that he can see me, but it still feels good.

Now I have to worry about running into him in my town. Luckily, I'll be busy at the ranch this week, so I'll do my best to push away my worries.

I'm on pins and needles now to get the hell out of

dodge. Dash is ready too. He's hanging his head out the window, enjoying the warm summer breeze—ears flopping in the wind. The corner of my mouth turns up watching him—despite the twist in my gut, knowing Kenzington is in my town.

8

DENTON

After a few hours on the road, the boys are restless. We stopped for coffee at a quaint little coffee truck, but they needed something stronger. They've been busy arguing over who forgot the cooler the last half hour, so it was time to find the bar in this town. I type bars near me into the maps on my phone. The closest one to the ranch is called the Wagon Wheel, and it looks like it's the only one in town.

We park the bus down a back street and walk to the bar. I take in the small cowboy town. There are a few shops, a diner, and the local bar, all surrounded by spectacular mountain ranges.

God, it's pretty here.

We follow behind Johnny through the old saloon-style doors into the bar. The place is dim and hazy. The bar is lined with stools that are made out of saddles. On the walls are pictures of old cowboys and cowgirls doing various western activities. It's the kind of joint where stories get louder and the night stretches longer. They have a badass stage that's calling my name. I love playing in cowboy bars.

Parker makes his way to the jukebox, and Johnny, Ray, and Grady get a high-top table near the entrance of the bar. I order enough long necks for each of us from the bartender.

As we settle into the worn-out stools, the doors swing open, and a rowdy-looking group of cowboys stalk in. The bartender starts pouring whiskeys and the group makes their way to the pool tables in the corner of the room. A tall familiar-looking cowboy is standing at the bar.

Johnny nudges me, nodding toward the bar where the familiar guy stands. It's Huck Kenzington and he's flirting with the sultry bartender.

"That's the guy you was jawing with last night over Sorrel, ain't it?" he mutters.

Parker, half-listening to the jukebox, catches the tension too. I nod, feeling the weight of the other night settle heavy in the air.

Things are about to get interesting as Huck cranes his neck, eyes raking over me. Sorrel isn't anywhere to be seen, but the air still crackles with tension. Huck Kenzington strides over, dark eyes and nostrils flaring, locked on me like a bull sizing up its rider. Which of us is going to last eight seconds?

"Got some nerve showing your face around here after the other night," Huck growls.

I stand to meet his height. He's maybe an inch

taller than me but his size doesn't intimidate me. I've taken on worse.

My grin tightens into a low smirk as I tell him, "She's nobody's girl, Huck. You're the one who's got a problem."

The room seems to shrink around us as we square off. Two men tangled up over a woman neither can claim, each carrying the weight of the fight like a loaded gun. Johnny and Parker exchange looks, knowing full well this isn't about to end with just words. Huck takes a step closer to me, and I take one too, filling the space in between us.

He puffs his chest out like a male rooster, ready to tear my eyes out with his claws.

My muscles coil like spring traps. I won't be the one to throw the first punch just like last time. Sorrel was the only reason I didn't throw a punch back—out of respect for her—but this time out of respect for myself, that shit ain't flying. If he swings on me, I'll be returning the favor. The bar goes quiet; even the jukebox seems to lower its volume in respect of the brewing storm.

Before fists can fly, Johnny shoves a hand between us. "All right, all right, let's all just take a breath here. We're here for a good time, not a hospital visit."

Huck snarls but backs off, still glaring at me. "Better not see you around here again, Reed." Then he turns and shoves his palm into the swinging saloon door. It swings hard back and forth; the soft creaking is the only noise in the bar as we all watch it.

Parker shakes his head, breaking the silence. "That was close. You okay, man?"

I run a hand through my hair, adrenaline still coursing through my body.

Letting out a shaky laugh, I say, "Yeah. I'm not sure this gal is worth this kind of heat. I'm not here to start fights."

I sure want to find out though. Is she worth it?

Johnny smirks. "Maybe next time, tell that to Huck before you open your mouth."

I turn to see his buddies are back to playing their game of pool. No one chases after or coddles him. Maybe they're tired of his antics too.

I'm itching to get the hell out of here and get to the ranch. I down the rest of my beer, the liquid cooling down my fired-up body. I slam the bottle on the table when I finish.

"Let's get outta here, boys," I say to the crew.

They all start chugging their beers. I sit back, letting the buzz hit me and hope it will calm my wild nerves.

We load up into the bus, the boys all whooping and hollering. They're in better spirits now and the stop did them good. We'll be to the ranch soon, where they can all let loose.

We climb the ridge that leads to the Saxxon Ranch. I stare out the window, overlooking the valley, and my mouth goes dry. I've never seen anything like it. The magnificence of it all, the lush green grass, and the small creek that runs through. It's like a work of art.

"What a beaut!" Johnny calls out from the back of the bus.

Ray pulls the bus through the large open gate, *SAXXON RANCH* on the overhead beam we drive under.

"You ready for this?" Ray asks.

I swallow, the taste of beer in my mouth sour now. Man, I could really use another.

I put on a face of ease and confidence and pat him on the shoulder. "Sure am, let's do it!"

9

SORREL

I'm putting the finishing touches on the guest cabin when I hear the rumble of an engine coming from down the road. Our guests were supposed to be here this morning, but no one had shown up. I was starting to worry they would be a no-show.

Squinting through the dusty windows, I catch sight of a big bus rolling in. A bus that looks way too familiar. It kicks up clouds of dirt as they slow near the barn, and my heart skips a beat when I spot the bold lettering along the side of the bus: *Denton Reed.* My insides plummet, seeing his name so bold and clear right here on my family's ranch.

No fucking way.

My breath catches as the door swings open and out steps Denton. There he is with that same charming smile and worn boots, but somehow, he seems more real here on my turf than under the bright lights of his stage. I blink, trying to process it—

wiping at the dust on the window with the rag in my hand as if what I'm seeing might be an illusion.

What the hell is he doing here?

Dad is walking out of the main house to greet them, and the one with wild hair that looks like he just rolled out of bed runs up to shake his hand. Denton catches me staring through the window, and I drop to the floor. My hand flies to my chest pounding.

I slowly rise, turning back to the window and peek out the bottom—he's laughing at me. I mean, I am hiding like a little girl who just got caught watching her crush. Even so, is this some big joke to him?

Who does he think he is, showing up here like this? I said no for a reason, and now he's here on my family's ranch. That's it, I'm ready to give him a piece of my mind. I throw the rag down on the floor in frustration, then walk out the front door and down the steps of the cabin. I stop inches in front of him and put my hands on my hips.

But then, the rest of the world fades away as we lock eyes. The bustling of the ranch, the other trucks, even the dogs barking in the distance. It all fades out, a strange feeling stirring inside of me. Excitement? Anger? Nervousness? Maybe a little bit of everything.

This is going to be a lot more complicated than I thought.

He looks me over like it's no big deal, like showing up here is just another stop on his tour. I stiffen, crossing my arms.

"Well, look who decided to crash the party," I say, trying to keep my voice steady.

Denton gives me that easy grin, unbothered. He lowers his eyes to my mouth, now smirking, like he knows something I don't.

"Well, it's good to see you too, cowgirl. Thought me and the boys would take a little vacation. No pressure, no big scenes. Just some quiet time and maybe a little cattle wrangling."

I raise an eyebrow, not quite buying the "no pressure" part.

"Right. And I'm just supposed to roll out the welcome mat?"

He shrugs, hands in his pockets. "I'm here to relax, not complicate things. Figured I'd keep it simple."

I study him for a beat, trying to read what he's really thinking.

Turning on my heel and heading toward the cabin door, I call over my shoulder.

"Well, don't get too comfortable. We've got a busy week ahead, and I'm not making it easy for anyone." Looking back over my shoulder, I make sure he's following. I catch a sly grin. He's laughing softly behind me.

"Wouldn't have it any other way," he says.

I whip around to face him at the entrance of the cabin, forcing a tight smile. "All right. Let's get this over with. Follow me."

Denton falls into step beside me like we're old friends. Like he hasn't just casually shown up at my front door with a tour bus and a smile that makes me barely able to stay upright every time he aims it my way.

"This is the guest cabin," I say, waving my hand across as if I were on a game show, showing off a fancy new car. "Five bedrooms, three bathrooms. Full kitchen and a porch with a view. Jo, our cook, will make all three of your meals per day. There are snacks in the pantry if you get hungry in between meals. You can leave any dishes in the sink and Lucy will get to them, but be respectful and try to clean up after yourselves." I spit it all out sounding like a drill sergeant.

Denton chuckles softly. "We ain't a bunch of heathens, Sorrel."

Ignoring him, I keep walking, boots clacking loudly on the hardwood floor in the silence. The rest of his crew tramples into the cabin like a stampede, laughing and slapping each other on the back like a group of teenage boys.

This is going to be a long ass week.

Denton introduces them all one by one. "This is Johnny, lead guitarist; Grady, bass player; Parker, drummer; and Ray, pretty much does it all and we couldn't do any of it without him.

"Hey, I'm Sorrel," I wave.

They all say, "Hi, Sorrel," simultaneously.

Dad walks in last, clapping his hands together to get everyone's attention. "All right boys, listen up. Sorrel will be your go-to person for the week but please don't use and abuse my sweet daughter or there will be hell to pay."

No one says a word back; all too intimidated by

him. Dad is a rough-looking old cowboy who wears a permanent scowl. He has salt-and-pepper hair and tan, wrinkled skin from spending most of his life in the sun. He only ever wears cowboy-cut Wrangler jeans that are always starched and pearl-snap short sleeves in the summer. He doesn't ever leave the house without his cowboy hat and a pocketknife strapped to his belt. He's as cowboy as they come.

He turns on his boot and walks out of the cabin, the sound of his starched jeans swishing back and forth.

Oh Dad, I sigh.

"Damn he's intense," says the one who I think is Grady.

I laugh under my breath and look out the window over the kitchen sink to see Johnny wandering toward the barn. He starts striking up a conversation with one of the ranch hands, pointing to his chaps and making big hand gestures. Denton walks up behind me, looking out the window. He shuts his eyes and pinches the bridge of his nose.

"Johnny can kind of be a handful, but I'll make sure I keep him in line."

Before I can respond, Parker, the one with curly hair and a round face, calls out.

"Hey, Denton, this place is badass. Do we get to ride today?" He's carrying two guitar cases and has four cowboy hats atop his head.

"Tomorrow," I say before Denton can answer. "You'll meet with me at five a.m. sharp to feed the horses and clean stalls. We'll have breakfast at six a.m.

and then we'll be moving cattle after breakfast. You'll need to prove you can handle a horse before I take you anywhere near our cows."

Denton smirks. "Looking forward to it."

Grady moans. "Manual labor at five a.m.—are you serious?"

I shoot him a sharp look and then aim it back at Denton.

"This isn't a beach vacation, Reed. I know you rodeoed in college, but it's different out here. Someone gets bucked off or trampled, they could get hurt badly or even worse, die. This is our way of life, and we respect it and the animals. It's not a show for us."

He raises his hands and leans back against the counter, crossing one leg over the other. "Hey, I'm not here to play anything. Just here to breathe for a while and get back to my roots."

My brows knit in response. Denton moves his face closer to mine, just inches away.

Lowering his voice, he says, "And by the way, I really like it when you get sassy and call me by my last name."

I can feel his warm breath on my neck, and goose bumps prickle my skin. He's flirting with me, making it hard to focus. I turn away, my cheeks red. I push off the counter and walk away—unable to ignore the way he sends electricity down my spine.

It's one week. I can get through it. Or maybe this entire week is going to be one big disaster.

"Just keep your boys in line," I say flatly, ready to finish the tour.

I leading him to the master bedroom, stopping outside the door while he wanders in. I sigh impatiently, looking down at my watch. It's already suppertime. Denton finally comes out of the master. He hasn't stopped smiling, acting as if he belongs here.

"Well," I say reluctantly, "Jo made enough food to feed a small army tonight. You guys better get some supper. Dinner is in the main house."

Denton's eyes light up. "Will you be at dinner?"

I bite the inside of my cheek before answering. "I'm not missing out on Jo's cooking. You better get some before it's gone." I leave them to unpack and get settled and make my way to the main house.

My mind still can't comprehend him just showing up here like this. I didn't even give him my damn phone number, so how the hell did he find our ranch?

Sure, I guess anyone with half a brain could google my last name and the ranch would pop up first thing. But never in a million years did I imagine Denton Reed would be one of our guests. Sure as hell makes it harder to suppress the feelings I've been trying to bury since the other night, and now I'm forced to face them.

There're too many emotions I need to face, and it all feels overwhelming. I don't want to feel anything. I want to sink into the numbness of it all—I'm so fucking tired. Emotionally, mentally, in every damn way. I'm not ready to go down that road again. Not even for a smooth-talking country music star with sparkling green eyes and a voice—God that voice. Every time he talks to me, I feel a heat spread through my entire body. I'm like a damn Roman candle on the verge of shooting sparks in every direction.

I felt something similar to that in the beginning with Huck, but never as intense and it stopped pretty early on. Sex had become a chore with him, and eventually, his touch made my body go rigid. I can't imagine being with someone in that way again. My body might be feeling its own type of way toward Denton, but my mind isn't. It feels like my body is betraying me. I don't know when—if ever—I'll be ready to be with someone intimately again.

. . .

A spread of Jo's delicious food lies across the long wooden table in the main house. Roast beef, mashed potatoes swimming in gravy, sweet corn, biscuits, and her famous peach cobbler already cooling on the counter. The smell alone is enough to make a grown man cry, and my mouth is watering.

Jo is bustling around in her apron, barking orders at my dad to stop stealing bites from the serving platters. She swats at him with a kitchen towel.

"Clint Saxxon, if you touch that cobbler, I swear I'll kick you out of my damn kitchen."

Dad just grins like a kid caught sneaking cookies.

"Worth it," he snickers.

Sutton, Ryder, and Trotter are already at the table when the front door opens and the boys pile in. They shimmy out of their dusty boots with wide eyes, taking in the warmth of the old house.

The main house was built in the 1980s and is still in its original form. It was built out of locally sourced logs and the wood is a warm rich mahogany color. It's as if each piece tells a story of history. My favorite thing about the house is the oversize stone fireplace that sits in the middle of the living room with Dad's elk mounted atop. We've had so many nights cuddled up on the couches and stories told in front of that fireplace.

Sutton snickers when she notices the guys taking off their boots, and nudges Ryder's elbow.

"No need for that, boys, you're in cowboy territory now and we don't take our boots off unless we're getting laid, in bed, or both," Ryder says to them all gruffly.

Not a single one of them respond, a look of surprise across their faces. Denton started to slip one boot off and shoves his foot back in before walking over to where I'm sitting at the table.

He pulls the chair out next to mine, and I fidget as he sits down.

"Evening, gentlemen," Dad says as he comes out of the kitchen. "Glad to have you boys here. Hope Sorrel didn't scare you boys too bad during the tour."

"She gave us the full drill sergeant tour," Johnny says with a grin, earning a toothy smile from Sutton across the table.

Denton gives a polite nod to everyone, and when he sees Trotter, his face lights up.

"Is this the Trotter I heard all about?" he asks.

"This is him, the star of the show," Sutton tells Denton, tousling Trotter's hair. He smiles up at her and then buries his face in her underarm. Apparently, he's feeling shy tonight.

Everyone piles into the food, and most of their plates are empty within a few minutes. Jo brings out seconds for everyone, muttering something about "grown men eating like starving coyotes."

It's loud, messy, and if I'm being honest, kind of fun. The boys are hilarious and have us all laughing so hard our cheeks hurt. Even Dad is chuckling a bit. Denton was right, and Johnny is definitely the more "flavorful" one of the group.

Sutton leans over to me mid-meal, and whispers in my ear, "That's *the* Denton Reed, isn't it?"

I nod.

She grins. "Well, damn, you could have cleaned up a little more, Sorrel."

I look down at my dirty jeans and quarter zip I have on. My hair is tied back in a braid, and the only makeup I put on this morning was a little concealer and blush. Denton overhears her, and is holding back a smile. I shake my head and take another bite of potatoes, pretending not to notice Denton's gaze continuing to linger on me like I'm the only one in the room.

"You don't need to clean up for me. You're beautiful, Sorrel," he says, so quietly I wonder if I imagined it.

I feel my stupid cheeks giving me away again. I

don't reply. My eyes drift to Sutton and Ryder. They are sitting close together, and their fingers brush as they pass the rolls.

The quiet way they look at each other—like the world could fall apart and they'd still be solid—makes something ache deep in my chest. I admire them more than they probably know. Their story isn't easy, but they made it out the other side just fine.

I glance back at Denton and catch him watching them too, a soft look in his eyes like maybe he longs for the same thing. When our eyes meet, he gives me a small, almost shy grin. I drop my eyes to my plate and clear my throat.

"Well," I say, pushing my chair back and standing. "If everyone's done stuffing their faces, we've got an early morning ahead of us. Cattle don't wait on hangovers or beauty sleep, so don't let me catch anyone bitchin' and moanin' when it's time to cowboy up."

A few chuckles ripple through the table, but I mean every word. Tomorrow is going to be a long one and I need to keep my head on straight.

Jo takes my plate from me. I offer to do the dishes, but she refuses. I need something to distract me.

I step outside onto the front porch. The ranch has gone quiet, the kind of quiet you only get way out here, where the wind hums through the pines and the stars feel close enough to touch.

I sit down in one of the old wooden rocking chairs, and it creaks as I stretch my legs out and close my eyes, taking in the day and how I feel about Denton being here. Here with me, and my family, at our ranch. One side of me is annoyed and the other…well, the other side feels happy.

It's a confusing feeling, one I still can't really wrap my mind around.

The band on the other hand seem laid back and it will be a nice change of pace. If I can just ignore Denton's flirting, the week might not be so bad.

I rock back and forth, taking in deep breaths, looking out over the dark pasture. Crickets sing their song and one of the barn cats slinks by, chasing shadows. Just as I start to stand to go back inside, I hear the screen door screech behind me.

"Didn't mean to interrupt," Denton says, his voice low and timid. "Mind if I join you?"

I hesitate, then shrug. "Our home is your home for the week."

He sits down next to me in the other rocking chair.

"This place is somethin'," he says, looking out over the land. "Feels real."

"It is," I reply, a little sharper than I mean to. "This isn't just a tour stop for us. This is our life."

He doesn't flinch. "I know. That's kinda why I came."

I side-eye him. "Still wrapping my head around that."

He gives me a half smile. "Look, I meant what I said earlier. I'm not here to make anything complicated. I just want a break from the noise. And maybe I wanted to see you again… but no pressure. Just bein' honest."

I stare into the darkness, letting his words settle in the quiet. "You know," I say after a moment, "people like you don't usually stick around places like this."

"Maybe I'm not people like me. You think you have me figured me out, Sorrel Saxxon?"

I don't have an answer for that. He's right. I don't know him, and I am unfairly categorizing him into a group that may not be him. But that doesn't mean I'm going to just take his word for it.

After a while, he nods toward the guesthouse. "Well…guess I'll turn in. Big day of cowboying tomorrow."

"You boys better get used to early mornings and sore muscles. You ain't rock stars out here. There's no partying all night and sleeping all day," I say with a soft smirk, trying to lighten up a little.

He grins as he turns to go. "That's why I'm here, Sorrel. Good night."

He walks away, leaving me here on the porch, alone with the stars and the annoying little flutter in my chest I don't want to admit is still there.

10

DENTON

We wake at the crack of dawn and follow the smell of fresh biscuits coming from the main house. Biscuits and gravy, crispy bacon, and scrambled eggs are out buffet style. We all grab a plate and dig in. If we keep eating like this, I'll be a few inches thicker by the time this week is over. Jo's cooking beats the hell out of the sad gas station sandwiches and energy drinks we usually live on.

I hoped the coffee I drank this morning would perk me up, but now I just feel anxious and jittery. Even with a full stomach and night of rest, I can't shake the nerves creeping in. I'm stoked for the cattle drive. I've been on the road so long I'm ready to be one with nature. No more bright lights and dark hangovers. My body needs a reset and I think this is exactly what will do it. But Sorrel has me all twisted up. I can't get a read on her. I thought we had a spark at the rodeo, that easy kind of connection that doesn't come around often… But maybe I imagined it. Or maybe the punch I took gave me a mild case of romantic dementia, who knows?

Either way, it's time to cowboy up. I'm not gonna be just some tourist playing dress-up. I want to prove to her, and maybe to myself, that I'm not just the shallow country music star she thinks I am. I'll make her see that if it's the last thing I do. Denton Reed is no quitter. I wouldn't be where I am today if I were.

I couldn't wait to get in the saddle. Sutton gave us a good berating for twenty minutes on safety and horsemanship. I was surprised she didn't knock Johnny upside the head when he pretended to get on his horse backward.

Sorrel paired me with a young mare named Whiskey. She's a cute palomino quarter horse on the taller side, but to my surprise she's mean as hell. Every time I ask her to move forward, she pins her ears and swishes her tail. One of the ranch hands promised me she was the best ranch horse they have, but I'm not sure I believe him.

The saddle creaks under me like it's trying to warn me—*quit now while you can.* I've rode horses before—broncs when I did rodeo, and putted around on my sister's old horse Tank. But this? This is a whole different experience. It feels like I'm driving a Ferrari, and I'm not sure which buttons are safe or which one might send me into launch mode. Lord help me.

The Montana sun isn't even high yet, but my thighs already hate me, and I'm starting to think my cowboy hat is more for show than shade. Up ahead, Sorrel sits her horse like she'd been born in that saddle. Quiet, focused, and heart-stoppingly beautiful. She pays me zero attention, focusing on the task at hand. I'm not used to that. I'm used to women looking at me like I'm the damn prize. But Sorrel? She doesn't bat an eye when I smile at her. Just keeps riding and ignoring me like I'm another tourist trying not to fall off.

"You cowboy's good back there?" Ryder calls back with a smirk.

I throw on a grin. "Hanging in there. Saddle's just gettin' to know me is all."

Everyone chuckles, and I let it roll off me. Humor has always been my go-to—it's like armor. But I can't stop the flicker of irritation in my gut. Not at Ryder. At myself. Because I don't like being the rookie. I don't like not knowing the rules. I built a whole career on looking like I have it all together, and out here… I'm all hat and no cattle. Literally.

Johnny rides up next to Sorrel and starts talking her ear off. That boy is a rambler, but maybe he can soften her up for me a little. Put in a few good words.

I keep catching myself watching them—trying to figure her out like a locked door. I don't know if I should knock or kick it in. She has a wall up, that much I can tell. It feels as sharp as barbed wire. And part of me knows I should leave it alone. She made it clear this isn't anything. I have to stop believing all the stories in my head that I call a love song. Real life doesn't work like that.

The cattle are already moving. Black Angus cows and their calves are winding through the rolling hills. All around I can hear the sound of saddles squeaking, hooves on dirt, and the low bellow of a calf calling for its mama.

The sharp whistle from a ranch hand brings me out of my daze. Sorrel starts calling out directions to the hands. She breaks into a trot, her long braid swinging behind her as she rides, catching the sunshine. She's so stunning. This isn't some hobby for her. It blows my mind that this is her life. Hard-earned, gritty, and unshakably real. Talk about actually living.

I kick my horse into a trot and catch up with Johnny and Parker, who are trying their best not to look like a couple of city boys flopping around on the back of their horses. They're definitely country boys, not cowboys. Grady trots up next to the rest of us. He looks like his ass feels the same way mine does. The saddle is riding him, and he's hurting.

"Man, I don't know how the hell people do this for a living," Grady says.

I smirk looking over at him. "Don't worry. Your ass will have enough calluses by the end of the week."

"I'd prefer my rear end to stay as soft as a baby's bottom. The ladies like it better that way."

"No girl cares about the way your ass feels, Grady," Parker cuts in.

"How the hell would you know?"

"Your bunk's under mine. I know exactly how many women you've brought on the bus."

"The both of you have gotten more action from your left hands than any women," says Johnny.

"Yeah, yeah, we all know you're the ladies' man, Johnny, no need to brag," Grady replies.

I just laugh and shake my head. Johnny has his shirt unbuttoned down to his belly button and jeans tucked into his boots. I have no idea how he pulls so many beautiful women. He is a ladies' man no doubt.

I see him making eyes over at Sutton and I nudge Parker to give him a smack.

"Ouch! What was that for?"

"Don't look at Sorrel's sister that way. She's a married woman," I tell him.

"Fine," he sighs. "What else am I supposed to look at then?"

I gesture to the land around us, but my eye catches on Sorrel. It's fucking impossible not to get lost in her beauty, but I force my gaze away and take in the scene before me.

The Saxxon Ranch stretches out in every direction like a picture on a postcard. It's hard to believe places like this really exist when you've been living in a concrete jungle for so long.

The mountains loom in the distance, quiet sentinels keeping watch over the valley. Wildflowers dance in the breeze along the fence line, and the smell of damp earth and grass fills the air. This place isn't just beautiful. It's alive.

There's something so freeing about it all. Out here, you can't fake it. The land doesn't care who you are or what stage you played on last. Either you ride or you don't. Either you work or you get out of the way. And I want to work. I want to be a part of this. If only for a little while—and maybe, just maybe, earn another look from the woman riding ahead of me like she owns the whole damn world.

11

SORREL

We direct our horses toward the watering trough for a quick drink. We've been riding for over an hour now and have only moved one herd to the south pasture. Two more to go, and these boys already look like they're hurtin'. City slickers in cowboy boots—bless their hearts.

Denton comes trotting up on his horse besides mine, his hat pulled low and sweat trailing down his jawline. Still smiling, still trying.

"Careful," I warn, nodding to his mare. "She's a nasty one. Tried to take a chunk out of Duke last week. Keep her in check."

"Yes, ma'am," he says with a crooked grin, tipping his hat as if he's auditioning for a Marlboro ad. "So, on a scale of one to full-blown disaster, how'm I doin'?"

"You're not dead. That's a win," I shrug. No need to boost his ego too much.

"That's it?" he asks, mock offended. "Not even a

half-smile for the guy risking heatstroke, chafing, and public humiliation for the full cowboy experience?"

I turn, finally meeting his eyes. Mistake. They're striking, and there comes that warmth again.

"This isn't a retreat for us, Denton," I say, the bite slipping into my voice before I can stop it. "This is our life. It's not about impressing anyone. It's about not screwing up and getting someone hurt." That one lands hard. His smile fades, and that easy charm disappears.

"Right," he says quietly. "Got it."

I shift in the saddle, guilt tugging at my chest. I'm being too hard on him. But this isn't a damn photo op. Out here, one wrong move and you aren't just embarrassed—you're in the ER or worse. Still...he is trying—a lot harder than the usual guests we get out here. I can tell he actually wants to learn this way of life.

"You're doing fine," I mutter, almost too low to hear. He looks over, doesn't smile. Just gives me a little nod, respectful, like maybe he understands a little more than I thought. As we're getting ready to move the next group of cattle, a shout rings out from behind us.

"Loose calf!" Larry, one of the hands, hollers in our direction.

"I got it!" Johnny shouts, spinning his horse in a circle like that's gonna do anything.

I whip around just in time to see a lanky black calf take off toward the thicket. It's running full speed across the open field, tail flagged high like it's damn proud of itself.

"Of course," I mutter, already turning Duke to give chase.

"I'll come with you," Denton says, kicking his mare into motion before I can tell him not to.

We break off from the herd, the sounds of cattle and hollering fading behind us as our horses pound across the pasture. The calf zigzags like it's being chased by the devil himself, but to my surprise Denton keeps up.

I have to admit, he rides better than I expected. A lot of bronc riders don't even know how to actually ride a horse—just get bucked off them. Denton rides deep in his seat, loose and balanced, not gripping the reins like his life depends on it. I'm sure his mare appreciates him not pulling on her face.

We manage to get ahead of the little bastard, cutting it off before it can slip into the brush. I ease Duke to the left, and Denton moves to the right, flanking the calf in a perfect little pinch move.

"Well, look at you," I say, unable to hide the flicker of surprise in my voice. "Real cowboy in the making." I wink at him.

"Oh, is that right? Don't you know, I'm as real as they get," he puffs. "I ain't no gunsel, Sorrel. But I will admit I'm mostly just praying this horse knows what she's doing."

I laugh, really laugh this time. It slips out before I can stop it. And damn if it doesn't feel good. He looks proud of himself for getting it out of me.

We slow our horses as the calf reluctantly trots back toward the herd, now trapped between us. The poor little guy knows he lost the game.

The wind kicks up a bit, ruffling Denton's shirt, and he gives me a look that isn't cocky or smooth, just a sweet smile that says thank you.

I look at him for a long second, then give a small nod. "Thanks for the help, cowboy."

We ride back in silence, but it's a comfortable one this time. The kind that settles in when two people feel comfortable enough that they don't need to fill the silence. Damn it, if I don't hate how easy it is to enjoy riding beside him.

As we rejoin the group, Denton peels off to help one of the hands close the gate behind the second herd. I swing down off Duke to tighten my cinch, brushing dust off my jeans and trying to ignore the wave of happiness that has settled in me.

Sutton walks over, leading her horse by the reins, and leans in close enough that no one else can hear.

"Someone's got a crush on the pretty country music star," she whispers with a smirk, nudging me with her elbow.

I shoot her a sharp look. "I do not."

She raises an eyebrow, clearly unconvinced. "Right. That's why you were grinning like a school girl after you and Denton were playing tag with that calf."

I shake my head, ignoring her. I make myself busy with Duke's mane, working the witches' knots out of it with my fingers.

"Mmm-hmm," she hums. "Stop trying not to feel anything. You're allowed to be happy you know."

Before I can fire back, she turns to mount her horse, leaving me there with the reins in one hand and my walls crumbling down just a little in the other.

DASH TROTS BESIDE ME AS WE WALK THROUGH THE west pasture, looking over a few broodmares with their babies. The air has cooled, finally, and the last blush of sunlight is bleeding off the mountains like a watercolor painting. I needed a minute to myself before dinner just to breathe. The quiet out here has always been a comfort. But tonight, it feels heavy. Like something is shifting.

As I walk toward the main house, I catch the sound of soft picking. The familiar rasp of guitar strings under calloused fingers. I pause.

Denton is sitting near the fence line, his long legs stretched out in front of him, hat tipped low, just picking a slow, wandering tune. He looks peaceful. It's almost as if the ranch is claiming him and his guitar. Like maybe he belongs here.

"That sounds beautiful," I say, stepping into view.

He looks up, not startled. Eyes crinkling at the corners.

"Didn't take you for the type to sneak up on a man while he's baring his soul to the mountains."

I snort. "That wasn't soul-baring. That was three

chords and maybe a lyric, but like I said, it sounds good."

He taps the guitar. "Gotta start somewhere."

I hesitate, then walk over and lean on the fence beside him. For a minute, we sit there side by side. Him strumming something low and sweet—me staring off at the last light fading across the ridge.

"I'm not trying to impress you," he mumbles, without looking at me.

I blink. "Did I say you were?"

"Nope. But I can tell I've been trying too hard anyway. Think I wanted to prove something."

I pause, not knowing how to respond to that. He sets the guitar down gently beside him.

"Truth is…I've been so burnt out. The music, the shows—I love it don't get me wrong. But somewhere along the way I forgot what I was doing it for. Then I got here…and it's like I remembered how to breathe again."

That throws me off balance for a beat. I look over at him. He isn't putting on a show. Not tonight.

"I thought this was just a vacation for you."

He smiles, soft and a little sad. "So did I."

I shift my weight. "You're not the only one hiding from a life you used to love."

He glances at me but doesn't push.

I exhale. "This place…it's safe…and I've been hiding out here most of the summer, hell, probably longer than that honestly."

He nods. "He hurt you."

I look down at my lap. "Yeah, he did."

He doesn't ask any more questions, just lets that comfortable quiet land again between us. After picking up the guitar again, he plays a few slow chords and hums something low.

"You writing a song?"

"Maybe." He gives me a sideways look. "Kinda hard not to with you around."

That gets a laugh out of me. "Am I gonna be your muse?" I ask, flipping my hair back and squaring up with him.

He shrugs. "I was thinkin' 'bout it, girl as pretty as you, how could I not make you my muse." He pauses again, then adds. "My agent called earlier. Big tour. Bigger than anything we've done, so I'm gonna need some new material."

"Wow, Denton, that's amazing. When is it?" I ask with genuine excitement for him.

"I told him I needed a few more days to think about it."

He looks at me then, serious. "This place, it's making me question things. And I don't know what that means yet."

My eyes go wide. "Denton, you've only been here one day and you're ready to trade your mic and stage for a meager ranch hand salary?" I tease. "I thought furthering your career is what you wanted? You said so the other night."

A muscle in his jaw ticks. "Yeah, well, maybe it's not. Maybe I want a quiet life, not always on the road with no real place to settle down. Maybe I want somewhere I can hide."

He looks serious, and I'm at a loss for words again. This man has a habit of doing that to me.

The sound of gravel crunching under boots pulls both our heads up. I turn, squinting into the fading light. It's one of the younger ranch hands, Crease. He's maybe sixteen, all legs and looks like he needs a few extra meals on him.

Dad hired him last summer. Crease had been giving his mom grief and getting into trouble at school. She lost her husband and he lost his father, so I don't really blame the kid. Everyone handles grief differently, and for him, it was acting out. But his mother was now raising four boys alone on one income. She didn't know what to do with Crease. So, when she called up dad and asked if he could come work at the ranch, he of course said yes. One summer and a hard winter were enough to straighten him out, though. He chose to keep living here, but Sutton says he gives most of his wages to his mom. Ranch life has a way of shaping young men and building character. He's proof of that.

Crease jogs toward us, hat in hand and breathing shallow from running.

"Uh, Miss Sorrel?" he calls.

I straighten. "What's wrong?"

He skids to a stop just past the barn, darting an uneasy glance at Denton before focusing on me.

"It's Sutton, says she needs you to come to the main house now."

12

SORREL

Denton and I walk into everyone gathered around the table. They all have grim expressions on their faces, and my heart immediately starts racing.

"What's going on?" I ask nervously.

"Sit down, Sorrel," Dad says. "Denton, this is family matters. You can go ahead back to the guesthouse with the rest of your crew."

"Just tell me what's going on."

Denton starts to turn around and our eyes meet. Something inside me wants him to stay. Whatever is going on is freaking me out. He must sense it because he stops and takes the seat next to mine.

Dad eyes Denton wearily. "Sutton, tell her."

"We got another court order from the Kenzingtons. They're coming after us, Sorrel."

I slam my fist onto the table. "Fuckers."

Denton already knows their son is a real piece of

work. He's about to learn the apple doesn't fall far from the tree.

"When's the court date?" Ryder asks next.

"Two weeks from today," Sutton says, sliding the paperwork to me.

The Kenzingtons are wolves in sheep's clothing. They have more money than they know what to do with, and word around town has been that they're trying to buy up as much land as they can throughout Montana. They know we would never sell. I guess that means they'll try to steal it from us instead.

The court order states something about a boundary dispute.

"Fucking bullshit," I say under my breath, tossing the paperwork back onto the table. It scatters in every direction. I can't stomach looking at it anymore. "They're trying to claim our ranch."

Denton puts a reassuring hand on my knee under the table, then realizing he's touching me, quickly pulls away. My head is spinning. I don't even have time to register how his touch makes me feel.

"That would mean at some point they had someone out here to survey our land," Dad says, scratching the back of his neck.

He's just as confused as the rest of us. It makes no sense. How in the world could they claim our ranch? Huck must have put them up to this. That's the only reason they would come after my family.

"We're gonna fight this. There's no way in hell it will stand," Sutton says to the group.

Everyone agrees, and I know I have some work cut out for me.

Ryder stands up from the table. "Anyone want to let off some steam after today? Lucy is watching Trotter for us, and Sutton and I are gonna head to the Wagon Wheel for happy hour."

I take my hat off, letting my braid loose, and run my fingers through my sweaty hair. "I'm in. I'll give Charli a ring."

"I'm sure the guys are all in too, they never turn down a happy hour," Denton says.

THE WAGON WHEEL IS DIM AND NOISY, JUST THE WAY I like it. I slide onto a worn stool next to Charli, the wood sticky beneath my palms. Ryder and Sutton are getting a round of drinks for everyone. Denton and his crew are at the pool tables, starting up a game.

The clink of glasses and low hum of country music barely register as I watch Denton, free and easy. Not even noticing that every girl in the bar is staring at him.

"God, Charli," I mutter, "I'm about ready to lose my damn mind."

Charli gives me a sideways glance, already sensing the storm behind my calm facade.

"What's eating at you this time, Sorrel? You've been tight-lipped ever since that handsome country music star showed up at your ranch."

I hesitate, then push the words out like a knife

slicing through a thick wall. "It's Denton. It's Huck. It's everything. I'm spiraling, Charli."

Her eyes soften. "You like him, don't you?"

She knows me better than anyone.

Denton is bent over the pool table, about to make his shot. His eyes lock on mine. A heat ignites low in my belly, and I chew on my bottom lip. Sutton brings our drinks over and takes the seat next to me, a grin playing at her lips.

When I look back at Denton, a girl with light brown hair has her hand on his shoulder while she whispers something in his ear. Her features are dark and alluring and everything about her screams sex appeal. Jealousy settles deep in my chest and I can't look away.

Charli turns her gaze to them. "You going to do something about that, Saxxon?" she asks.

I grip the glass in my hand tighter and grind my teeth. I let out a deep breath. "No, he's a single man. He can do what he wants."

But then he shrugs her hand off his shoulder and her face turns into a look of disbelief. The corners of my mouth tilt up.

A screeching noise comes from the microphone on the stage that catches all of our attention. Randy, the owner of the bar, is on the stage fiddling with the microphone. He taps on it a few times and clears his throat.

"Well, folks, we have a special guest that so kindly offered to put on a show tonight. Everyone give Denton Reed a warm welcome to the stage."

Denton looks stunned as a mullet. He gives me an accusatory look.

I put my hands up in innocence. "It wasn't me."

Charli starts slinking away, her body melting under the table. Our heads whip in her direction.

"You!" we shout at the same time—catching her red-handed.

"Look, I might've made a call when Sorrel invited me to the bar tonight and told me y'all were comin'."

Oh, Charli. It's too late. Everyone in the bar is staring at Denton, and Johnny has already run up on the stage, strapping a guitar to his back.

Denton throws up his hands, accepting defeat. "Fuck it, live in the moment and all that. Right?"

Cool confidence washes over him as he takes center stage. He definitely belongs up there with that mesmerizing smile he gives the crowd. They begin to play, and every girl in the bar damn near falls to their knees—including me. But out of everyone in the bar, his eyes only meet mine. Not the pretty girl who probably asked to take him home tonight, but me.

My lips part, and I feel my blood pumping. I shoot back my whiskey and get to my feet, making my way to the back door. I need to cool off. Charli calls after me as I push my way through the swarm of people at the stage but I ignore her.

As I open the back door, cool night air slams into my face, and I let out a shaky exhale. I lean against the fence and close my eyes, just for a moment. I can't have these feelings for Denton. It terrifies me. I can't get hurt again; my heart can't take another beating.

I sense a presence coming toward me, and my eyes shoot open. As my vision comes back into focus, the unmistakable, staggering figure of Huck fills the open space in front of me. His eyes are wild and glossy as he takes me in.

"Well, well, well… if it ain't Sorrel Saxxon, hiding and running away like you always do."

He's close enough I can smell his rank breath that reeks of liquor. It repulses me, and I choke down a gag.

We're outside alone, just the two of us; the noise dims around us. My heart slams against my ribs, and all the color drains from my face. I desperately look past him at the door to the bar—safety—but he blocks my path forcing me to stay put. There's nowhere to go and my back is up against the fence. He moves in closer.

"Huck, let me go. Now," I say through clenched teeth.

The tendons in his neck pulse as he sneers at me. His face is so close that our noses are almost touching.

"You ain't goin' nowhere, Sorrel. You're mine. When are you gonna get that through that pretty little head of yours? No one else can have you except me."

Turning my face, I flinch. "I'll never be yours," I whisper.

His hands are reaching for me. But before he can grab me, a large hand grabs him by the shoulder, hauling him away.

"Don't you fucking touch her!" Denton growls. Huck twists out of his grip, turning to face him.

"You again," he says, baring his teeth.

They reach for each other and begin to struggle. Next thing I know, everyone in the bar is pouring out around us. Johnny jumps on Huck's back.

Luke, Huck's friend, comes out of nowhere and is pulling Johnny off Huck. Charli swoops me away from the fight. Blows are thrown left and right. It's an all-out brawl.

The bartender comes out carrying a wooden bat, slamming it on one of the outdoor tables. "Break it up now! I'm calling the cops," she yells. Len is behind her moments later.

Everyone is running through the now open back gate, hopping into their pickups and taking off before more deputies arrive. Dragging Huck away, Luke saves his ass once again.

Denton limps over to where Charli and I are hiding.

A flash of bright truck lights aims toward us. The truck is driving straight at the open gate—engine revving. It turns at the last minute before they plow through the fence and us.

"This isn't over!" Huck slurs, pointing a finger at Denton as they drive away.

"Okay, someone needs to get that guy in AA and anger management asap," Johnny quips, like we weren't all just about to get ran over.

"Fucking Kenzington, I'm calling him in before he kills someone," Len says to the bartender as they turn and go back inside the bar.

I swallow my fear and stand, voice steady despite the pounding in my chest.

"You're hurt. Let me help you," I say to Denton.

He takes a step forward, favoring his left leg.

Charli's hand is still tight in mine. "I'll be okay," I reassure her.

She nods, giving my hand a squeeze. "I'll let Sutton know you're heading home."

I give her a nod before she turns and goes back inside the bar.

Throwing Denton's arm over my shoulder, we hobble over to my truck.

"What about your crew?" I ask him.

"They can get a ride back with Sutton and Ryder."

"Okay, I'll drive—"

"No, ma'am, you drank. My right leg still works. I can drive."

He's right. I probably shouldn't be driving.

We slide into the pickup in silence and Denton turns over the key, the engine roaring to life. A velvety blanket of darkness settles over the town. I've driven this road more times than I can count, but it never gets any less eerie at night.

When we approach the exit for the ranch, I tell him to go left instead of right. He doesn't question me just does as I say.

"Park up here on the hill."

He puts the truck in park. It's too dark to see the gorge below, where if you kept driving, you'd plummet into nothingness. It would take weeks, probably, before anyone would ever find you.

"I like to come up here sometimes when I need to get away from it all. It overlooks a steep, rocky valley."

I started coming here after everything that went down with Kenzington. I needed a place where I could be alone and be able to sit with my grief. It's no less crushing now than it was then. It floods my chest like a flash flood—no warning just rushing water ready to swallow me up.

"Are you okay?" he asks softly.

I laugh, a short, ugly sound. "No. Not really."

"When I saw him, towering over you—God, Sorrel, you looked so scared." He swallows. "I wasn't going to let him hurt you again. I saw him come into the bar and he watched you go out the back door. I had to get to you. I don't know what happened between you two, but I know it was something. When you're ready to tell me, if ever, I'm going to be here for you, Sorrel."

I feel something in me unfreeze a notch. I've been holding it in for so long. The shame and guilt I've felt over the past year isn't something I'm sure I'm ready to tackle yet. But for some reason, Denton feels safe. I want him to know my hurt so he can understand why I've been so cold toward him. That it isn't him, but it's something broken inside of me.

13

SORREL

We sit in the pickup, windows down. Crisp air and the sound of the wind rustling the pines fill the cab. I think back to that night. I've tried to erase it from my memory—I want so bad to forget it ever happened. The words cut like razor blades as I try to get them out.

"I thought he loved me. I made every excuse in the book for him."

Denton just gives me a look that says it's okay and to keep going. And I bare it all to him.

One year ago

We were in another one of our breakups when he showed up at the ranch, determined he was going to get me back.

It was cold and gloomy that evening. We were outside by the arena when the rain started coming down. We were arguing back and forth. He begged and pleaded, said he would change. It would be different this time.

I gave in to him. We ran into the barn to take cover from the storm.

He grabbed my face, pressing his mouth to mine.

It was passionate and soft at first. I missed him, and his touch, the feel of his hard muscles beneath my hands.

He pushed me up against the haystack.

Our kisses became more frantic and intense. I knew what it was leading to.

My skin was wet from the rain, and my sundress was soaked through. I ran my hands through his wet hair as he slid his hands up my damp thighs. He began to slip his fingers into my underwear.

"Not here, someone could walk in," I told him.

Anyone of the hands could have walked in or even worse, my dad. But Huck wasn't listening. He kept going. Caught in the heat of the moment, I knew he was needy.

It wasn't the right place and I didn't want to get caught with him in the barn. He had been pushy before, but nothing like this.

It was a matter of seconds before he turned me around and bent me over the haystack. His grip on me tightened, sliding my dress up with his free hand.

"No one will come in. It's fine, baby," he promised.

I gritted my teeth and gave in to his needs.

He loves me. He's my boyfriend. He wouldn't hurt me.

His thrusts were hurried and he wasn't gentle in the slightest, but he finished quickly.

After stuffing himself back into his jeans, he kissed the side of my head. One tear rolled down the side of my cheek as I pulled down my dress.

I'm unable look at Denton while I tell him what

happened between me and Huck, but I know he's listening the entire time. Tears are running down my cheeks. He holds my hand in his, letting me try to get the rest of the words out.

After that night, I couldn't look at Huck the same. I cried myself to sleep that night, staring at his back, while he slept peacefully.

I knew then that he had no idea what love was. That putting your needs before someone—who you supposedly care about—is wrong.

It was a few nights after that when I discovered he was cheating on me.

I should have known he wasn't the faithful type. I couldn't have felt more stupid and disgusted with myself.

Instead of hurt, I feel anger as I tell Denton the rest of my story.

. . .

We had stayed up drinking and fighting all night before the rodeo. We both felt horrible the next day.

We didn't talk to each other the entire drive, occasionally pulling off to sleep before we finally made it to the arena grounds.

It felt like the longest drive of my life. I stayed in the car feeling sick and tired and didn't get out until he was up to ride.

I sat on the fence line and took my phone out to record.

He drew a nasty bronc.

He got into position on the horses back. Pulling his hat down low, he nodded and the chute opened. The bronc busted out of the chute, bucking and snorting. Huck was spurring him when he lost his seat, getting bucked off. He got hung up in his riggin, the bronc dragging him around the arena. With pure terror in my eyes, all I could do was watch as the bronc trampled him. The pickup men were doing their best to get his hand out, but before they could, I heard a gruesome cracking noise.

My stomach churned and adrenaline pumped through my body as I jumped the arena fence, heart racing, running for him.

His leg was broken at the ankle, and turned out in the wrong direction. His cowboy boot was the only thing holding it in place.

I held back the bile rising in my throat, trying to stay strong for him. It hurt my heart to see him in so much agony and pain, even after what he did to me.

He screamed with a rage that frightened me.

"FUCK! I'm done. This is going to ruin my fucking season."

I'd never seen him so angry.

The paramedics loaded him onto the stretcher and into the ambulance.

I told him I would follow behind the ambulance to the hospital and call his mom to let her know what happened. As I backed out of the ambulance, they began to close the doors.

"Don't you fucking call her and don't go through my phone." He screamed at me as the doors shut in my face.

I had no idea what all that was about and stared at the ambulance in confusion as they drove away.

When I got to the car, I opened his phone, and all the evidence was right there, bright as day.

That good-for-nothing prick. Not just one but multiple women, including his ex. I scanned through dates and thought back to our relationship timeline. The cheating wasn't even when we were broken up.

I pulled over to the side of the road and vomited. Screaming and crying, on my hands and knees, I let it all out.

He broke me. My heart was in a million pieces. I didn't know how I could go on. But day after terrible day I did.

. . .

I take a long, deep breath when I finish telling Denton my story. He looks at me with sadness and a look of understanding in his eyes.

"I'm so sorry, Sorrel, thank you for telling me."

I nod, wiping away my tears.

God, I'm a mess, and I can only imagine how I look right now.

"Every time I see his face, the memories come rushing back in—they flood my mind and I—I feel like I'm drowning."

"Tell me what I can do to help."

"I wish there was something, Denton," I say, smiling softly and lowering my eyes. "It's something I'll hold with me for the rest of my life, but I know I'll overcome it."

It feels good to tell him. I've been holding it in for so long. It felt like someone was sitting on my chest, and now—the weightlessness—I can finally breathe again.

After that night, it was like I'd had an awakening. I woke up that morning and looked in the mirror. I didn't see the bright-eyed cowgirl who loved life. I had become a shell of my former self. But now, I'm reclaiming my strength.

I'm a cowgirl through and through, and as much as it hurts, I will face my demons. I'm done hiding and I'm done hiding who Huck really is.

14

DENTON

Morning comes quiet and cool. A silence spreads throughout the house that settles deep after a storm. The sun isn't up yet. I tiptoe out onto the front porch—leg still a little sore from tweaking it in the fight.

My heart feels heavy with the weight of last night. I want to fucking kill Huck Kenzington. I watched Sorrel struggle through her story, hands trembling as she recounted everything he did to her. It was almost too much to hear. I could see how badly it hurt her to say it. I wanted to hold her in my arms and take away her pain.

He took a woman so powerful and beautiful and tried to grind her down until she was nothing but dust underneath his boots. The bar fight plays over in my mind—Huck's rage, Sorrel standing tall even when she looked like she wanted to break. I realize now why she had been so cool toward me. I can't blame her for having her guard up. She's still healing and needs to face the damage he caused. I'll give her the time she needs and I'll be here for her through it all.

She reminds me of a sweet dandelion that someone stomped on, but dandelions aren't weak. They're strong and resilient, and with a little water and sunshine, they perk right back up.

IT'S AS IF SORREL HAS COME BACK TO LIFE AGAIN OVER the past few days. Her smile is brighter and her shoulders stand taller. She looks like the weight of everything has lifted off her and I'm sure as hell happy that I was the one she confided in.

It's our last day here on the ranch, and the week has flown by. My agent is still nagging me to make a decision about the tour we were offered. I'm so damn torn. I don't want to let the guys down. I'm not the only one who has been working toward this. But I've grown accustomed to ranch life over the last week.

Every morning over the past week we woke before dawn. Hot coffee and breakfast were ready to go and we were horseback the rest of the day. There was always work to be done—fixing fences, doctoring calves, you name it. The fact that I got to do it all with Sorrel just made it that much better.

Sorrel and I started up a routine, and every afternoon we would have our lunch together on the porch of her cabin. She'd pop her boots off and cross her legs beneath her while I swung us back and forth on the porch swing. Dash would sit underneath her, begging for food, and we'd both throw him a couple of bites and chuckle. It was all so peaceful, and I'd grown to love the familiarness of it all.

No loud and rowdy crowds or bright lights. Just staying in one place and learning more about myself than I ever knew was possible. But I figured the others would be eager to get moving—tour life calls for speed, and these boys won't linger in a place this slow for much longer.

I took my time getting out of bed this morning—it being the last day and all. By the time I wandered out of my room, Johnny and the rest were already packing up, ready to roll.

Ray is back to pick us up in the bus, waiting on us all to load our gear.

"Hey, you guys heading out?" I ask Johnny.

"Yeah, I think we've had enough fun playing cowboys," he jokes.

Jo walks in with a bunch of to-go containers filled with all kinds of baked goods. She loved how much Johnny could eat and she sure kept him fed all week.

"JoJo baby, I sure am going to miss your cooking," he says with a wink and nod in her direction.

"You come back anytime and I'll take care of you." She smiles big.

God, he's such a flirt. I shake my head and laugh.

I start toward my room to pack my things, but then I spot Sorrel out of the corner of my eye, through the open door as she's riding up on Duke. She sits tall in the saddle, eyes sharp but tired. When she calls me over, I can sense something is wrong.

I walk out onto the porch and she's standing there at the railing, fidgeting with the reins in her hands.

"You leaving?" she asks, voice low and timid.

"Our week is up—figured you'd be kicking us out first thing. The boys all said they're done playing cowboys."

She nods, a little stiff. "You weren't playing anymore, Denton."

"No, ma'am I wasn't," I say, no hesitation.

There's no gleam in her eyes but there's something honest there that makes me want to stay—even if I'm not sure what I'd be signing up for.

"I could stay," I blurt out.

"You got your tour to get back to. I have a few rodeos coming up, anyway. I won't be around much longer," she says, looking away from me.

"Then I'll go with you. Are they pro rodeos? I have a contact so we can play at any pro rodeo. I never agreed to tour, Sorrel."

"You have to, Denton. You're meant to be a performer. This life is too slow for you. You'll grow complacent and hate it here eventually."

Part of me knows she's right, but there's something worth exploring between us. I just can't leave yet. I look at the guys loading up, ready to get on with their lives, but my boots feel rooted here.

"Hey, y'all, listen up," I shout in their direction. "Head home for a while, spend some time with your families, play some smoke-filled bars in Nashville like old times, and I'll call when we got a gig lined up. I—I can't leave here just yet," I stutter.

They all look at me with understanding.

Ray gives my shoulder a squeeze as he walks past me and into the bus.

Fuck, I feel horrible. I haven't even told them about the tour yet. Was it wrong of me? Yes. But I will eventually. I just need a little more time to get things sorted out. This isn't just about proving to Sorrel I'm not Huck. It's about being somewhere real. Somewhere I can finally stop running.

. . .

I don't waste any time after the others leave. I grab some gear and head straight to the barn.

I figure if I'm going to prove myself, I better get my hands dirty. Sorrel will see I'm serious about this way of life and that I can slow down. I'm not going anywhere yet.

Jo's breakfast is still settling in, but the smell of hay and leather is exactly what I need to be around. I find Sutton and Ryder already at work, fixing a fence near the north pasture.

"Morning, Denton," Ryder calls, wiping sweat off his brow. "Ready to earn your keep?"

"More than ready!"

Ryder grins, handing me the fencing pliers. "Good man. We'll put you to work."

The hours pass fast, filled with fence repairs, feeding cattle, and even wrangling a stubborn colt that refused to be caught. Sorrel was nearby, watching but not saying much. I catch her eyes a few times, and each time, there's a flicker of something—curiosity?

Maybe a little respect? I can't quite put a finger on it.

We take up our usual lunch spots. It feels different this time, partially because I'm supposed to be gone, and I think she wasn't expecting we'd be here together again today.

"I'm not easy to figure out," she says quietly. "And I have trust issues."

I nod. "I'm not here to fix things overnight. Just to show up and show you I won't just walk away."

She glances at me, a small smile breaking through. "Well, you're doing better than most."

Maybe this really could be the start of something real. That little flicker of hope ignites and continues growing in my chest.

15

SORREL

Sitting by the bonfire, I stare into the flames. The orange glow flickers shadows across my tired face. Everyone has gone to bed and the ranch is quiet except for the occasional snort from the horses in the barn. It's moments like this that I feel the weight of the world settle heavy on my shoulders—all of my emotions weigh me down.

This week felt like it had been an entire year with everything that happened. My mind wanders, and I continue to wrestle with my feelings for Denton. How could we ever make something work? Sure, the ranch could survive without me, and in the winter, I could be on the road with him. But what about rodeo—would I be willing to put barrel racing on the back burner?

The rodeo circuit isn't just a hobby. It's in my blood, my soul. It's years and years of hard work and time spent in the saddle. Training my horses with my own tears, sweat, and blood. I love chasing the rush, the freedom of the arena, the feeling of triumph when I win a race. It isn't glamorous—it's gritty, hard, and unpredictable. But it's mine. It defines me.

If I hypothetically were to explore something with Denton, would I let his dreams come before my own? He's a different kind of wild. His life is packed with flashing lights, screaming fans, and endless tours that span across the states. His world is chaos wrapped in melodies and sold-out shows. The kind of life that demands your time, energy, and emotion, leaving little room for anything else.

He may want to slow down now, but something in me tells me he can't stay still for too long. But I want to believe maybe there is a middle ground. That two worlds so different can somehow collide and coexist. I just don't want to fall and he be gone before he can catch me.

When Huck came into my life, it was a wild ride that left me broken and wary. Denton's kindness and the way he's been here for me has made my heart grow in a way I wasn't expecting. But what good is putting my heart on the line if it means losing myself in the process?

I don't want to be just another stop on his tour. I don't want to put my life on pause, waiting for a call, a text, a chance. I need to be whole. Strong. And right now, that means choosing the ranch, rodeo, and my healing.

Maybe one day the stars will align. But tonight, as the fire goes out and there's nothing left but hot coals, I push the thoughts and feelings away. I remind myself to stay focused. Because some dreams—no matter how much you want them—aren't meant to be chased at the same time.

I'VE BEEN DREADING THIS DAY FOR WEEKS. THE DAY WE face the Kenzingtons in court over our ranch they're trying to steal out from under us. I tossed and turned all night long, thinking about how it would go. Then, I found myself headed to Denton's cabin in a moment of weakness. But luckily as I tiptoed to the door, Dash caught me sneaking out. As he stared up at me with his head tilted in question of where I was going, I knocked some sense back into myself. I scooped Dash into my arms and crawled back into my own bed, where I belonged. Sleep never really came and the bags under my eyes are proof of that this morning.

I look down at my phone to a FaceTime call from Mama. I answer, putting on as brave of a smile I can muster.

"Hi, mama!" I say as the call connects.

"Hey, buttercup, you almost to town? Sable is here with me. Say hi," Mom says.

"Hi, Sable butt, I miss you. When are you gonna come cowgirl again with your sisters?" I ask, teasing her.

She rolls her eyes. "Once I'm done with this extra course, I'll be coming back out to the ranch. How's Daddy doing? Is he coming today?"

"He's good. He misses his baby girl too, but he

knows you're out there living your big city girl dreams. He wouldn't miss it. When someone comes after what's his, he means business."

Dad has been fucking livid ever since we got the court summons. I'm surprised he didn't show up at the Kenzingtons with a loaded shotgun and handle it the old-fashioned way.

"I don't know who these people think they are messing with your daddy's ranch, but I'm sure they have no idea what's coming for them," mom says, putting her face so close to the phone I can't see Sable anymore.

"That's for damn sure. Uh…by the way, I'm bringing a friend. He's in the truck with me now, so don't say anything embarrassing, please," I say under my breath.

I look over at Denton, who insisted on driving me to Billings today. Dad drove Sutton, Ryder, and Trotter in his pickup, so there wasn't enough room for all of us in his old Dodge Cummins.

When Denton noticed I was driving alone, there was no chance he wasn't coming with me. He grabbed my keys out of my hand and hopped in the front seat before I could protest. Dash tried to jump in too, but I told him he had to stay at the ranch with the other dogs today.

It's going to be a long day, and my nerves are all over the place. I'm actually grateful Denton offered to drive and I don't have to be alone for the next few hours trapped with my anxious thoughts.

"OOOOOH, Sorrels' got a friend that's a boy?" Sable says mockingly.

Mom mouths to her, "*Quit it.*"

Sable's been giving me a hard time since she was born. Said it was her job being the baby of the family.

"Okay, love you, bye!" I quickly hang up the FaceTime call.

I turn to Denton, my cheeks red. "I'm going to apologize for them in advance. They're two peas in a pod and always getting into trouble."

He chuckles softly. "So, if you don't mind me asking, why don't they live with y'all on the ranch?"

"Mom and Dad got divorced when I finished high school. She said they were still best friends, but the romance wasn't there anymore. Dad was always working on the ranch and I think it came first a lot. I think she kind of felt like she was raising us alone if it wasn't ranch-related things."

"Gotcha, and Sable wanted to go to college in the city?"

"Yep, MSU, she's getting a degree in creative writing. We've all always loved to read and write since we were little girls."

"I get that. Writing songs is one of my favorite things. It forces me to face my emotions and not hide from them."

That strikes me right in the chest and I feel a slight twinge. Clearly, his comment is aimed at me. I nod and turn up the radio, not wanting to get into it with him. I take three deep breaths in and four breaths out. A breathing technique that will supposedly reset my nervous system, according to Dr. Morgan on Instagram. I know I probably shouldn't take medical advice from doctors on the internet but I'm desperate to calm my frayed nerves.

I'm praying Huck isn't in court with the Kenzingtons today. Early mornings aren't really his thing, so I don't think he'll show. Unless his parents drag him out of bed and force him to go.

We park in the parking garage for the courthouse. It's amusing seeing our pickups all backed into these tiny spots and not any other trucks in sight. They sure don't consider country folks when they spray the parking spots in these garages. do they?

I spot Sable's strawberry-blonde hair pop out of her GT Mustang and Mama is getting out of the passenger seat. Sable springs into action, running for me and jumping into my arms. She's always been the more affectionate one out of all three of us girls. She looks like she just stepped out of a magazine, wearing a two-piece blazer set and short kitten heels. Her outfit blows mine out of the water. I'm wearing a plain black dress that has little silver buttons through the middle and flats. I threw my hair up in a claw clip, thinking maybe it would make me look a little more sophisticated for court.

"Oh my God. Is that Denton Reed?" she whispers in my ear.

I nod and give her a raised eyebrow to play it cool.

She shoots out her hand. "Howdy, I'm Sable, the funnest Saxon sister out of the bunch. It's nice to meet you."

He tips his hat and shakes her hand. "It's nice to meet you too, Miss Sable. I've only heard good things."

He turns to Mom. "Ma'am, I'm Denton. It's a pleasure to meet you."

She shakes his hand and my mom actually blushes. I swear I've never seen her blush in my entire life. My mom is five feet eight inches with dirty blonde hair the same color as Sutton's. She's a tall drink of water. Even as she ages, she continues to grow more beautiful than ever. Today she has on dress slacks, a satin button-up shirt, and heels that make her even taller.

The rest of the family is unloading out of Dad's pickup now, and Dad comes around the back and stops dead in his tracks when he sees Mom. She turns to him, and they give each other a big hug, and dad kisses her on the cheek. Even though they're not together anymore, I know they still have love for each other. Trotter runs up to Denton and jumps up and down with his arms in the air, wanting him to pick him up.

"Hey, traitor!" I say playfully.

Denton lifts him into his arms. Seeing him hold my nephew makes me weak at the knees. I wonder if he wants kids. He sure is good with them.

Sable and Sutton are walking with their arms locked, and Denton, who's still holding Trotter, and I stroll behind. Being with all my family like this makes me feel whole and fills me in a way that I didn't know was missing.

"You've got an amazing family, Sorrel," Denton tells me, giving me a genuine smile.

"I sure do."

I look at each one of them, and my chest aches from how much I love them all. I know how important the ranch is to all of them and it would break us to lose it.

Dad stops in front of us and turns around, taking his cowboy hat off. "Well, guys, I just want you all to know that no matter what happens in the courtroom today, I love each and every one of you from the bottom of my heart—except you, Denton—no offense, but I just don't know you that well."

We all laugh, and I shake my head. "Anyways, this ranch has been in my family for eight generations. The Saxxons are fighters and that's exactly what we're gonna do today. Those Kenzingtons are gonna learn they fucked with the wrong family."

On that note, we're all fired up. We go into the building, my heart hammering in my chest.

16

DENTON

We were in court for nearly six hours. After three of those hours, we discovered the Kenzingtons have been buying up small parcels of land around bigger ranches for years. They would purchase senior water rights and file a "corrected survey." After that, they were able to manipulate easements and access to the river beds.

Somehow in the mumbo jumbo fucked-up world of laws and ownership they could claim the rights to that property. It's what's called a boundary dispute. And the Kenzingtons are so slimy they just hope the owner of the ranch doesn't notice. Eventually, no water equals no ranch.

Over time they set up a claim to the land and take possession of it. That's exactly what they did to the Lazy C Ranch. It took a couple of years but eventually they got away with it.

Now they thought they could do the same thing with the Saxxon Ranch.

Luckily Sorrel is on top of her shit and caught them right away. It turns out she was onto them months ago. God, she was mind-blowing in there. She radiated confidence and had done her research. She had every piece of paper the judge—who was clearly in on it with the Kenzingtons—asked for. Surveys, title records, and public findings. The judge tried to refuse some of the evidence—I think Mr. Saxxon had some dirt on him—after he went up and had some private words with the judge, he straightened out real quick. Gotta love small towns.

I could tell the Kenzingtons' betrayal hurt Sorrel more than she let on. She confided in me that Mrs. Kenzington started to feel like a second mom to her when they were together. She said Huck and his dad were the conniving ones and that she actually felt sorry for his mom. I could absolutely believe that.

When Huck and I college rodeoed on the same team, his dad was always real hard on him. Always rubbed the other parents the wrong way. I felt bad for Huck until I realized he was just like his father. Just because your old man is a dick, doesn't mean you have to be one too. I would know. But damn if I didn't try to be his friend when we first started school. He was always a great bareback rider but it was his cocky attitude that always got him in trouble. Clearly he never changed.

I'm waiting out in the hall for them to finish up, checking a few emails when I get a text from my buddy about performing at a pro rodeo this weekend.

I start up a group FaceTime call with the guys to make sure they're all in. I'm sure they're itching to get back on stage.

"Hey, y'all, there's a pro rodeo in Great Falls this weekend. The Big Sky pro rodeo. It's three days and we got offered to perform every night. Y'all in?"

"I'm in," Parker says while he's brushing his teeth in the background.

Johnny pulls his wild dark hair out of his face. "As long as Sorrel's hot friend is gonna be there I'm in," he chides.

Grady chimes in next. "She's way out of your league, dude."

"Yeah right, she totally wants me. We'd make the cutest little tan babies together."

Johnny has a mischievous grin on his face. I look over my right shoulder and see Sorrel is standing behind me.

"Did you guys know she was there the whole time?"

They all start laughing, Sorrel too.

"Well, I guess you have some matchmaking to play," I say to Sorrel and then look back at my phone. "All right y'all better be ready this weekend. I gotta go." I hang up the phone and smile, looking up at Sorrel.

"What's this weekend?" she asks.

"We just got an offer to perform at the Big Sky rodeo all weekend. Are you gonna enter?"

"I'm entered," she says, giving me a smirk.

The corners of my mouth turn up. "And you weren't gonna tell me, were you?"

"Nope, figured you were playing anyways," she says, walking away, changing the subject. "So, the rest of the family got hotel rooms to stay in town tonight, but I want to get back to the ranch since I left Dash. I can drive—"

"No, it's fine. I'm good to drive."

My stomach dips thinking about Sorrel and I being alone at the ranch together. There's always been someone around so it's been difficult to get any alone time with her. We would have over an hour car ride home and the rest of the night alone. I can't deny how excited I am to be around her some more. Especially just the two of us. Still, I'm not trying to rush anything with her. I know the kind of trauma she's been through isn't the kind of thing you just get over.

Something similar happened to my sister and it didn't just hurt her, it hurt us all. It took years of therapy before she was able to start dating. Hell, I probably should have gone to therapy too. The anger and hate I felt in my soul took time for me to move past but music helped. I wrote a song for my sister and it was healing for all of us. I'm a huge advocate for women who have been in similar situations and I do what I can to give back. Any man who does something like that to a woman is no man in my eyes. They're the scum of the earth. I just wish the legal system were better. If it were up to me, I would have taken things into my own hands and gotten justice for my sister—but I'd probably be in prison right now—and I've learned that you have to let the victim handle it how they want. You can't force anything on them. I know her situation is different from what happened to my sister. But it still doesn't make what Huck did okay. So, I'll do the best I can to be there for Sorrel—even if it's never anything more than just friends.

On that thought maybe she doesn't feel comfortable being alone with me? Maybe I ought to let her drive herself home.

"Are you sure you're comfortable with me driving you home alone tonight?"

"Uh yeah, just said I was. Why? Am I gonna find out you're like Garth Brooks and everyone thinks you're actually a serial killer?"

I start full-blown belly-laughing. "People think he's a serial killer?"

"Yeah, there's a whole Reddit thread about it. Let's just say I went down that rabbit hole one day, and honestly, I think they might be onto something."

"Well, I'm not a serial killer. I just want to make sure you're comfortable, that's all."

She purses her lips in thought. "I do feel comfortable with you, Denton."

And there goes my heart again.

Sorrel asks all kinds of questions as we drive home. Everything from wanting to know about me and my family, to being on the road and performing in honkytonk bars. Anytime I try to turn the subject back to her, she changes it again and asks more about me. Her curiosity's peeked and I think she's trying to figure me out. If she doesn't know by now, I'm an open book. I tell her everything she wants to know.

"So how are you feeling now that all that legality stuff is over? Was it hard seeing Kenzingtons' parents again?" I ask, finally getting a question of my own in.

We're almost back to the ranch now. Lightning strikes in the distance and it looks like a storm is coming in. There go my plans of sitting out on the porch with her all night. I want to know how she's feeling before she can run off into her cabin.

"I feel relieved. I hope it will get him off my back. Part of me wishes Huck would have been there so I could see the look on his face when he realized they lost. But truthfully, I'm glad he wasn't there," she replies.

I feel my jaw clench when I think about him being anywhere near her. I tried to be the nice guy with him but I'm threw with that shit. Something in me feels protective over Sorrel now. I probably don't have the right to be but I can't deny the feeling. If he comes near her, I don't know what I'll do next.

"Honestly, Sorrel, if he doesn't quit harassing you, I think you might have to file a restraining order."

"Look, Denton, I don't need you to get involved in my drama any more than you already have. I'm a big girl and I can handle myself."

My grip tightens on the steering wheel. Her reaction confuses me.

"Hey, I got involved by default and I'm not trying

to tell you what to do. Just trying to give you some advice, Sorrel."

"Yeah, well, I don't—do you see that smoke?"

We're curving around the last bend of the mountain, and down in the valley is a cloud of smoke growing bigger by the minute.

"That's the ranch! Hurry up! Drive faster!"

I put my foot to the floorboard driving as fast as I can down the dirt road. The gate is open to the ranch, which is strange this time of night. There's a small fire in one of the fields and the hands are already working on putting it out. They have the water truck in the field spraying water all over the fire. It looks like they have it under control but I still wonder if I should call for help.

"Oh thank God," Sorrel says, putting her hand to her heart. "Drive up to the barn. I want to check on the horses."

As we veer around to the barn, Sorrel opens up the truck door before I can even blink and jumps out while we're still driving. I slam on the brakes. She's frantically screaming for help as she runs but no one is around to hear. All of the hands are in the west field putting out the first fire we saw.

I throw the truck in park, running after Sorrel. She's almost to the barn. The building is engulfed in flames. She runs straight in before I can stop her.

I follow her in shielding my face from the smoke and flames.

"SORREL! Where are you? Sorrel!" I scream for her but I can't see her through the smoke.

Clint's office is to my right, and I try to turn the door handle, but the knob singes the skin on my palm. I kick with the heel of my boot over and over again until I kick the door down.

The fire hasn't spread to the office but Sorrel isn't in there. Fear pierces my chest—if anything happens to her—I can't let my mind go there right now. Staying cool under pressure is what I do.

I can do this.

I spot the red fire extinguisher and grab it before running farther into the flames.

I spray at the flames trying to clear a path. The smoke drifts away for a mere second. At the other opening of the barn is the silhouette of a figure in black wearing a cowboy hat. I can't see who it is.

"Help! Please help!" I beg.

They take off running in the opposite direction.

Smoke begins to fill the barn again. I continue spraying, running through the barn looking in each stall when I finally see Sorrel. She's in Duke's stall trying to coax him out. It looks like she got all of the other horses out, but he's spooked and won't leave his stall.

I run over to them still spraying with the fire extinguisher. Sorrel is trying to lead Duke by his jowls and I spray at the fire around them. Breathing is becoming difficult and I can feel myself losing oxygen.

Duke rears back as I spray and it all happens so fast. The fire extinguisher goes empty. Duke is on his hind legs, and when he rears back, he hits Sorrel in the head knocking her unconscious. He runs over her limp body, missing her by an inch. I crouch down to try and pick her up but I feel so weak. I take cover over her as pieces from the barn begin to fall.

"Sorrel..." I wheeze and begin coughing. I can't get enough air into my lungs.

Next thing I know the world goes black.

17

SORREL

B*eep..beep..beep.*

I try to pry my eyes open but they won't stay put. Every time they open, I see flashes of white. They flutter closed again. I try opening them again. I see a blurry face. I hear beeping noises. *Where am I?*

"Honey, are you awake?"

I think I am.

This time I open my eyes and they stay open. My throat burns and my head hurts.

"My head hurts," I say to whoever is standing above me.

"Okay, I'll call the nurse, darlin'. Don't move."

Darlin'. Must be Dad.

"Where are we?"

"We're in the hospital. Do you remember what happened? Actually, don't answer that. It might make your head hurt worse. Where the hell is the fucking nurse?"

"Is she awake?"

I hear a high-pitched frantic voice.

"Why didn't you tell me she's awake? Sorrel, Mama's here, baby."

I turn to see Mom. She's holding clothes, a hair-brush, and a makeup bag.

"I brought your stuff so we could fix ya up a little. Oh, thank you Jesus for waking up my baby girl."

"Thanks?" I rasp.

The nurse comes in now.

"Fucking finally," Dad says.

The nurse checks my vitals. "Hi, hun, we're going to get you taken care of. I already let the doctor know you're awake."

"My head hurts," is all I say back.

"I'll get you something for your head and the doctor will be in soon."

The nurse leaves the room. Mom and Dad are both staring at me with pained looks on their faces.

"So, is anyone gonna tell me what happened?"

Mom comes over and takes my hand in hers. "Honey, there was a fire. You got knocked unconscious trying to get Duke out."

It all comes rushing back to me. The fire. Huck in the barn with a can of fuel spreading it around. Me trying to get the horses out. Denton trying to help me.

Wait, Denton was there.

"What happened to Denton? Is he okay?" I ask frantically.

"I'm okay Sorrel."

I hear his voice from the corner of the room. It's

raspy and quiet but it's him. I crane my neck up to see him sitting in a chair in the corner of the room.

"He's been here the whole time, Sorrel," Mom says.

"Yeah, refused to leave to even take a shower." Dad rolls his eyes.

"Everyone else is in the waiting room. They only let three of us in here at a time, but we've all been with you, waiting for you to wake up, sweetheart."

Mom brushes my face gently and tears start welling in her eyes.

"I'm okay Mama." I give her hand a squeeze.

She turns around to hide her tears from me.

She takes a deep breath before saying, "You're okay." Mostly to reassure herself, I think.

Dad gives me a gentle kiss on my head before putting his arm around Mom, leading her to the door.

"Let's give them a minute," he whispers to her.

Denton comes over to the side of my bed and takes my hand into his. He holds on so tight like any moment I might slip out of his grasp.

"God, Sorrel, I was so scared you weren't gonna wake up." He clears his throat, holding back tears. "They said you had a concussion and they were going to keep you asleep to make sure you didn't have a brain bleed. The last three days felt like a lifetime."

"It's been THREE DAYS? Fuck, we missed the rodeo."

He lets out a hoarse laugh that turns into a fit of coughing. "You don't need to worry about that right now, Sorrel. Just focus on getting better."

I give him a sad smile. "Well, I ain't getting my entry fees back. And your voice—is it gonna be okay?" I ask concerningly.

"Doctors say they don't know, only time will tell…"

"God, Denton, I'm so sorry. I feel awful. This is all my fault."

"It's not your fault, Sorrel. They said it was a freak accident. Natural combustion or something like that."

"No–it was Huck! I saw him! He had a can of fuel. He started the fire!" I say too loudly, reaching for my throat as it feels like hot coals are being poured down.

Rage spreads across Denton's face. "The ranch hands pulled us out and the fire truck got there before it could spread, but the barn is gone, Sorrel."

My heart cracks. The barn used to be my favorite place. Huck ruined it for me and now he burned it to the ground. But in a strange way, hearing that, I feel relieved. Set free. I'll never have to look at it again and think of that night.

"We'll build another one," I tell him and pull my blankets up over my neck, a chill coming over my body.

"Why would they think it was natural combustion? There was a fire in the field so obviously someone had to have started both."

"I guess there had been a lightning storm that night before we got to the ranch. I remember seeing it in the distance as we were driving but didn't think anything of it."

In the summer, fires are caused by lightning from time to time, so it's not uncommon. It's also the perfect alibi.

"It wasn't lightning. It was Huck. I saw him do it."

"I believe you," he says, giving my hand a tight squeeze.

Knock knock knock.

"Charli!" I yell too loudly, my throat burning again.

She comes running over and jumps on top of me. I give her a big hug and breathe her in. She smells like honey and her tan skin is glowing.

"Well, you sure look a lot better than me," I quip.

"Oh, stop it right now, Sorrel! You're beautiful and you're alive! What the fuck, Sorrel, I was so scared. Don't you ever do that to me again!"

I let out a raspy laugh. "I'll try not to get caught in any more fires I promise."

"Good. Now where's that makeup bag your mama brought? Let's get you cleaned up. Denton, she's awake now and we need some girl time. Out." She points to the door with a hand on her hip.

I raise my shoulders and mouth, "Sorry."

"I'll be back in an hour," he promises me.

Charli helps me get up to wash my face and brush my hair. My skin looks so dull and dry. It's like the fire has shriveled me up into a raisin. I truly am grateful to be alive though.

Luckily most of the horses had been turned out to pasture so only six horses were in the barn when the fire broke out. When I couldn't get Duke out of his stall, I thought I was going to have to leave him to die in that fire. I never would have forgiven myself if he had died. He's my heart horse in every way possible and I want as much time with him as I can get.

I'm still in shock that Huck did this. I shouldn't be thinking about it right now but enough is enough. It's time for him to pay for all the hurt he's caused me and my family.

I'm sitting on the hospital bed while Charli does my makeup when I hear a squeal. I open my eyes to see it's Sable. We hug and cry and then she helps Charli finish my makeup that I've now ruined with my tears. I tell them everything that happened. Charli suggests we give her dad a call to get some advice on what to do from this point forward. He's a detective and a damn good one.

I go into details of that night only telling him about the fire and how I saw Huck starting it in the barn. He tells us to make a report with the sheriff's office ASAP and they should have him in cuffs by tonight. Let's see his parents try to get him out of this one.

A FEW DAYS LATER, I'M FINALLY DISCHARGED FROM THE hospital. I can't wait to get home and see Trotter and Sutton. Because of Trotter's age he wasn't allowed to see me in the hospital and he's been asking for Auntie Sor Sor, Sable told me. I tried to FaceTime him but I've been in and out of sleep the last few days. The fire took a toll on my body and every time I called Sutton or she called me, one of us was taking a nap.

Denton stayed with me for the rest of my stay in the hospital other than for his doctors' appointments. He has a nasty burn on his hand from trying to open Dad's office door. Thank God he got that fire extinguisher or I'm not sure we would have made it out. If his vocal cords don't heal, I'll never be able to forgive myself for getting him into this mess. What will he do with his life? I try not to let my mind go there. He seems to be in good spirits about everything so I'll try and stay positive.

I'm so excited Sable is back at the ranch right now and I guilted her into staying and taking care of her poor sick sister. She's going to stay in my cabin with me to help me while I'm recovering. I laugh to myself when I think about her and Denton bickering over who's going to take care of what. They've been going at it while I was in the hospital. She's a little fireball. Whatever man marries her will never live a boring day in his life.

I let Denton drive me home from the hospital since it will probably be pretty chaotic with everyone home at the ranch now. We won't get much time alone, which I'm kind of disappointed about. While we're driving, he reaches over for my hand. I don't stop him. I look up at him and give him a small smile.

"I'm really happy we're both still here, Sorrel."

"Me too." I rub my thumb back and forth across his hand while we drive the rest of the way home in silence.

His voice is still rough and it hurts him to talk. I'll make him Mama's tea recipe when we get back to the ranch. It's kind of like a Starbucks medicine ball with way more honey. She would always make it for us any time we had a sore throat growing up. That makes me wonder if he let his family know he was in the hospital. Did they come visit him while I was asleep?

"Did you tell your family what happened?"

"No, I didn't want to worry them. My mom would freak out and hop on the first plane here."

That makes me smile, knowing he has people that care for him.

"Yeah, I don't blame you. I'm sure my mom was a total mess when she got to the hospital."

Denton chuckles and side eyes me.

Oh gosh, I bet she went psycho on all of the nurses and doctors. I don't even want to know.

When we pull into the ranch, there's a deputy's truck parked in front of the main house. I assume he's here to talk to both me and Denton. Sable is sitting with the deputy on the porch. When we walk up, it almost feels like we're interrupting something. I give her a sly smile.

"Hello, I'm Deputy Ryan. Len sent me out to get your statements about the night of the fire."

I frown and wonder why Len didn't come out with him.

We both shake his hand and take our seats in the rocking chairs while he pulls one over to face us. Sable slinks away taking one more glance at deputy Ryan.

"So, please explain in detail what you remember from that night."

We both do our best to explain the sequencing of everything that happened. There are some fuzzy parts but I know without a doubt who set the fire.

Deputy Ryan scribbles in a notebook while we recount the night.

"So, you're saying for a matter of fact, this was Huck Kenzington who started it?"

"Yes, I saw him with the fuel can. Starting it with a lighter and continuing to spread the fuel all over the barn."

"And you? Can you say for sure it was him?" he asks Denton.

He rubs the back of his neck. "I saw someone in a cowboy hat—black one—but I didn't see their face."

"All right, well, that should be enough to bring him in."

We look at each other and our faces light up.

"Thank you so much Deputy Ryan. Please keep us posted," Denton says as they stand and shake hands again.

"Will do. Sorrel, take care of yourself. Try not to worry too much. We have your backs."

He tips his hat before leaving and his eyes wander over to Sable who's walking out of the pasture with Dad's old rope horse, Cowboy. My lips roll inward, holding back a smile, seeing there's clearly something there between them.

When he's gone, I sink into the chair and let out a long breath. Knowing Huck will be behind bars and can't cause trouble for us anymore makes me want to cry with relief. I think Denton feels the same way too, because the expression on his face looks a little lighter as we rock back and forth in silence.

My gaze lingers on where the barn used to be. It's nothing but ash now. Dad's office and who knows what documents were in there—all gone. Tack and saddles, all of it lost to the fire. But the horses are safe—turned out to pasture now. My heart twitches when I look back at Denton. He's watching me with a hazy smile. I'm so grateful to be alive, and here with him.

18

SORREL

It's been a month since the fire. Construction for the new barn started yesterday. We poured a new pad on the opposite side of the arena and the new barn will have an even bigger tack room and an office for me. It's going to be a completely fresh start and a totally different layout.

Denton helped us design the layout. Apparently, he had taken a few architecture classes when he was in college and he still has a good eye for it. I've been trying to keep him busy while we recover. I can tell he's starting to go stir crazy.

Today is Sunday so most of the hands are off and went to town. Denton and I are the only ones left at the ranch. Mama and Sable went home two weeks ago and Sutton finally quit mother-henning me after I begged Ryder to make her stop. He took her and Trotter into town to go shopping and get ice cream, and Dad decided to tag along.

Denton's voice is starting to sound a lot better and

we're hopeful he'll make a full recovery. We were both finally feeling good enough to ride today and I planned a trail ride to show him the secret waterfall we have here at the ranch. The waterfall is a special spot deep in the creek where, after a good rain, the water runs cool and clear, pooling just right for a swim beneath a gentle cascade. I've never shown it to anyone before. It's our family secret but I thought Denton deserved something special after everything we've been through.

I hesitate for a moment before knocking on the guest ranch door. The door swings open, and there he is—holding two steaming cups of coffee.

"For you," he says, handing me a mug with that laid-back smile of his.

We walk over to the rocking chairs on the porch and settle in gently rocking back and forth. The only sound around us is the creek of the wood and birds chirping. The morning sun, warm on our faces as we sip our coffee.

"So, how are you feeling now that Kenzington is going away for a long time?"

I think on it for a minute before answering.

"I'm glad his parents finally did the right thing by not bailing him out. But we still don't know how long he'll get."

"He'll get what he deserves, Sorrel, trust me."

"Yeah, well, I guess we'll find out at his trial. But for now, I feel safe. Especially with you."

He smiles softly in response, taking another sip of coffee.

"Ready to ride, cowboy?" I ask him, taking the cup from his hands.

"You know it, cowgirl," he says with a twitchy grin.

I leave the coffee cups on the porch railing and we head over to my horse trailer. The horses are already caught and tied to the trailer waiting for us. They greet us with sweet knickers.

We saddle up and get on our mounts. I steer our horses in the direction of the creek. The sun is higher now, filtering through the towering pines and casting dappled shadows across the dusty trail.

I let Denton ride Zip today, giving him a break from his sassy mare he's been stuck with since he first got here. It's good to let the barrel horses be ranch horses too. It makes them that much better in the arena.

The smell of pine and fresh earth fills the air and I take in deep breaths. It's nice not to have the smell of smoke singeing my nostrils anymore. The quiet around us is broken only by the soft clip-clop of hooves and the distant tinkling call of a meadowlark. The sweet song it sings fills my ears and makes me smile.

As we ride, Denton stays close, matching my pace. It's been weeks since I've felt any sort of calmness settle over me. I meant it when I said I felt safe with him. But I want to know more about him. That's what I was trying to do before the fire—actually get to know him—who he really is.

"So, you never talk about your dad. Is he in your life?" I ask him as we ride along.

He looks away into the distance like he's remembering something.

"No, he's not."

I'm not sure if I should push any further but then he continues.

"He was abusive to my mom and my sister. I fought him when I was sixteen. I'd had enough of it. Never saw him again after that."

"I'm sorry Denton."

"My mom and my sister are everything to me. We didn't need him," he says and shrugs.

My heart aches for him. I can't imagine not having my dad in my life. If I ever lost him or he had left us, there would be a gaping hole in my heart that could never be filled. I wonder if Denton feels that way, but he just doesn't want to admit it.

He goes on to tell me about how much he misses his mom and sister, and how he plans to take them skiing in Telluride this Christmas. There's a softness to his voice, a side of him I haven't seen before when he talks about them.

"Do you want a family?" I ask nervously.

It feels like such a deep and intimate question to ask.

"I do. Do you?"

"Definitely. Sutton and Ryder are goals."

"I agree," he says as he starts humming and smiling.

"It wasn't easy for them though. I admire them for making it. They've been through a lot."

"Like what?"

"All of it. Their relationship, marriage and then once they finally figured all that out and were ready to start a family, they struggled with infertility. It was hard on their marriage and even harder on Sutton. I was worried about her for a while."

"That's awful. I know people really struggle with that. It's cruel to want something so bad. More than anything in the world and not be able to have it."

"It is, but they fought and fought and now they have our boy, Trotter. I'm so proud of Sutton. She kept her faith and prayed for that little boy. She never gave up."

He listens, really listens, like every word matters. There's something so easy about talking to Denton—like I could sit here every morning, riding side by side, just the two of us. No pressure. No past hanging over us. Just two people sharing pieces of their lives, one ride at a time.

The waterfall comes into view now. There's a narrow ribbon of water flowing over moss-covered rocks into a clear blue pool. The world seems to hold its breath here, as if time slows just enough for us to catch it.

Denton dismounts and stretches, running a hand through his hair. "This is something else," he says, eyes bright.

I nod, feeling nervous and excited all at the same time to show him my special place.

We tie up our horses to a nearby tree. He turns his back as I shimmy out of my jeans and unbutton my shirt. I'm in nothing but my bikini now, feeling so vulnerable. I chose a pink two-piece set with little flowers all over the top and bottoms. They're cheeky and show a bit more than I'd like but it seems like that's how they make them now days.

Denton slides off his boots and pulls his T-shirt over his head. I admire his muscular back for a moment before he turns back to me. His green eyes go dark and a look of hunger and desire spread across his face. I smile shyly, taking him in too. His build is lean and abs ripple across his tan stomach. Warmth fills my core and I move quickly toward the creek—needing to cool off.

We settle onto a sun-warmed rock at the edge of the pool, dipping our fingers into the water. Denton glances over at me, his expression softer than before.

"You know I didn't come here to cause trouble. If I would have known what it could stir up, I never would have put you through any of it," he says quietly. "I just wanted to find a little peace. Maybe… maybe find something—I don't know…," he trails off.

I look at him then—a man who carries the weight of fame and expectation, who somehow made space for me in his busy world.

I shake my head. "None of it is your fault, Denton. I'd go through it all again just to be here with you."

He looks surprised. Like maybe this is the start of something neither of us expected.

Denton leans back on the rock, letting out a slow breath. "You know, I always thought this kind of quiet was boring. But here? It feels like the only place I can really hear myself think."

I smile, tracing circles in the water with my fingertips. "It's easy to forget how loud the world gets. Out here, it's just the land and the animals. I love being here after the hustle and bustle of rodeo season. There's nothing like being home after being on the road. I'm sure you know that."

"Kind of," he says, his voice unsteady. "I don't really have a home the way you do. I've got an apartment in Nashville I share with my band, but it's just a place to crash between shows. It's not the same as your home. I wish I had what you have."

His words land heavy. I glance at him out of the corner of my eye. He isn't smiling now; he's staring at the water like it's holding something he can't say out loud.

I wonder how it would feel to never really belong anywhere. To always be packing up, leaving, chasing another crowd. I feel a twinge of pain in my chest for him—for the boy behind the microphone, the one who maybe just wants a place to call his own—somewhere that isn't temporary.

"Home's not just a place," I say quietly. "It's people. It's roots. It's knowing you can come back."

He gives me a small, almost grateful smile.

"I guess that's what I'm still looking for."

He turns to me, eyes serious. "Sorrel, I know I'm just passing through your world, and you've got your own battles. But I want you to know—what I feel for you. I want more than the spotlight and the noise—the feelings I have for you are so much more real than all of it."

I swallow, the knot in my chest tightening.

"Denton…I want to believe that. I really do. But what about the tour, your dreams? I can't let you give up on it all to chase me around this ranch and the rodeo circuit. I'm tied to this life, to this land. Rodeo, the ranch….it's all I know. What if you get bored here and grow to resent me for not chasing your dreams? And what happens when you're gone and I'm left behind."

He reaches out, brushing a stray strand of hair from my face. "I'm scared too. But maybe we don't have to figure it all out right now. Maybe we just take it one day at a time. You teach me this world of yours, and I'll show you a side of life you might grow to enjoy."

I look into his eyes and feel something shift inside of me—hope, maybe, or the fragile start of trust.

"Okay," I whisper. "One day at a time."

"Yeah?" He smiles and leans in close.

I breathe in the scent of him—warm and comforting. My breath hitches, my heart pounds. I freeze up in a way that catches me off guard. Just as his lips hover near mine, I can't help myself—I splash water into his face and jump into the cool creek.

A look of surprise flashes over his face as he wipes away the water. "Oh, you're gettin' it now!" He laughs, shaking his head before plunging in after me.

The cold water shocks me awake, but the sound of his laugh makes me smile—happy, carefree, and full of hope. We both surface, water dripping from our hair, the sun warm on our skin. The sound of the creek rushing and our quiet laughter entangling with it surrounds us.

He grins, water sliding off his face. "You're impossible, Sorrel Saxxon."

I smile back. "Maybe I just don't want you to get too comfortable—gotta keep you on your toes."

He gives me a knowing look, then settles back against a smooth rock, letting the water carry him gently. I ease in beside him, the coolness soothing the heat that has been building between us all day and the heat that is now between my thighs.

We almost kissed.

Fuck, why did I chicken out and splash him? He's right. I am impossible.

The walls I've built since he got here are starting to crumble and I'm beginning to welcome it with open arms. Hell, we almost died. Life is too short, and it's time I finally admit to myself I'm falling for him.

And in that quiet moment, surrounded by the beauty of the land and the rush of the water, I lean over and kiss him. His lips are warm and soft, gentle yet demanding in a way that makes my heart race. Time seems to slow, the world narrowing down to just us. Even the soft sound of the waterfall behind us has faded away. His lips on mine are the only thing I can comprehend.

When we finally pull apart, I catch my breath,

eyes locked with his—both panting and fervent with need. We're interrupted when a few rain drops sprinkle on our faces. We look up, more drops begin to fall, until the sky opens up in a sudden summer downpour. The warm sun vanishes behind thick gray clouds, and the steady roar of the waterfall is soon drowned out by the patter of rain on leaves and leather.

I hope that isn't a bad omen.

I start laughing as I look up at the sky and Denton looks at me like I'm crazy.

"We better get moving," he says with a grin, putting my hand in his and pulling me up.

We scramble up the slippery rocks, slipping and sliding on the wet earth. Denton pulls on his shirt while we run for the horses. My jeans are soaked wet and there is no way I can get them back on. I tie my button-up around my waist so my ass won't be rubbed raw on the ride back.

The horses whinny, sensing the change in weather, and we hurry onto their backs before the storm gets worse. We break out into a full run across the field. I feel so alive smiling from ear to ear. Denton looks like he's hanging on for dear life and I can't stop laughing at him.

"Let's go, cowboy! Catch up!" I call out.

He pushes Zip harder and our horses run side by side.

By the time we put up the horses and reach the porch to my cabin, we're soaked to the bone. I'm shivering—but still smiling.

"Want to warm up by the fire?" I ask, my voice shaky.

"Sure."

A slight smile tugs at his lips. He follows me inside, and I busy myself trying to get the fire going. I turn my head looking back at him—his clothes are dripping wet, and all his things are back at the guesthouse.

"Let me see if I can find you something dry to wear."

I feel him step up behind me. Slowly, I turn around to face him. His eyes catch mine, dark and intense, before he leans in and kisses me. Electricity shoots through my body, melting the cold away, leaving only the ache of wanting him. My hands slide beneath the hem of his shirt, lifting it over his head.

"I don't want you catching a cold," I say, a little breathless, tossing his shirt onto the floor.

"You either," he whispers.

His fingers find the knot on my waist I tied my shirt in. He works at the knot as he gently brushes his fingers against my belly. When he finally gets it off, I shiver and look down at my wet shirt on the floor. He lifts my chin up looking into my eyes.

It's been such a long time since I've been with anyone—the last time was the night I've tried to forget. My mind is all over the place, but deep down I know what I want. And I want it with him.

"We don't have to do anything, Sorrel. We can just cuddle up by the fire and talk, watch a movie, whatever you're comfortable with."

The fire crackles softly, casting flickering shadows

across the room. His hands are warm against my skin, steadying me as if to say everything is okay—that this is safe.

"I want you," I say breathlessly.

Our lips crash together again, slower this time, savoring the taste and the feel of each other. I wrap my legs around him and run my fingers through his hair. I can feel him hard beneath me and his body shudders under mine. We break apart for a moment—he looks so beautiful, his green eyes bright, his hair slicked back but curling up at the bottom and dark from being wet. He smiles at me, a full toothy smile, showing the dimple on his left cheek that I rarely see. In this moment the weight of everything else disappears—the past, the hurt, the fear—fading away like ash off a fire. He traces the line of my jaw with gentle fingertips, his touch reverent, as if discovering something precious.

"Bedroom's that way," I whisper, nodding to the room behind me.

"I want you here," he says as he picks me up and carries me toward the fireplace. Gently laying me down on the faux fur rug.

The world outside disappears; all that matters is the soft glow of the fire, the warmth of his body, and the steady rhythm of our breaths. I stretch my arms out as he devours my body. The rough wood is cool against my palms, grounding me.

Every kiss, every touch, is a promise—not just of desire, but of something deeper. I close my eyes and let myself be here, fully and completely, finally giving in to what my body has been craving for months. We move together slowly, with care and urgency tangled as one. There are no words, only the language of skin and heartbeats, two souls finding comfort and connection in the quiet heat of the moment. The storm continues to rage outside—the whole ranch could be washing away, but we'd never know, so consumed with each other, nothing else matters.

When the fire dies down to embers, we lie tangled in each other's arms, the silence between us heavy with unspoken promises.

19

DENTON

The soft knock on the door stirs me awake. I blink against the morning light filtering through the curtains, Sorrel still tangled in my arms.

"Morning, beautiful." My voice is husky, a gentle smile tugging at the corner of my lips.

Her eyes slowly begin to flutter open. Before she can respond, knocking comes again from the front door.

"Just ignore it," she says, pulling me into her, but the knocking doesn't cease, louder this time.

Sorrel groans, untangling herself from me.

"I'll get it. You stay here," I tell her.

I wrap a blanket around my waist and pad to the door, then pull it open to find Sutton standing there, a mixture of amusement and disbelief in her eyes.

What the fuck was I thinking opening Sorrel's door half naked? Thank God it wasn't her dad or I'm pretty sure I'd have a shotgun pointing at me right about now.

"Dash got out again," she says, wrangling the squirming dachshund by the collar. "And he somehow made it all the way over to our place. Is Sorrel in there?" she asks suspiciously.

I glance back over my shoulder.

Cheeks flushing, Sorrel pulls on my shirt, her hair a wild mess of blonde tangles. I give her a wink as she comes to stand next to me.

Sutton's eyes flicker between us, a knowing grin spreading.

"Well, well, looks like I'm not the only one enjoying some company this morning."

Sorrel groans softly. "Sutton, it's not what it looks like."

Sutton laughs, stepping inside. Sorrel takes Dash from her. He licks her face, little tail going a million miles a minute.

"Relax, Sorrel. It's about time you two stopped pretending there's nothing between the two of you."

I start laughing, turning it into a fake cough as Sorrel gives her sister and then me a dirty look.

I shrug and then put my hands up. "Guess we got caught," I say as my blanket falls to the floor and I stand there, butt-ass naked in front of the Saxxon sisters, absolutely mortified.

Sutton doesn't even bat an eye, just laughs. "Don't let her scare you off," she says, shutting the door behind her.

I turn to Sorrel, embarrassment written all over my face. Her sister just saw me naked.

"Don't worry about her. Dad made her live in the bunk houses one summer with all the cowboys when she went through a wild phase in her twenties. She's seen it all, trust me."

"I still don't want your sister seeing all my goods."

"Your what?" She bursts out laughing.

"Yeah, my goods, I know you remember them from last night, darlin'," I say with a wink.

She throws a pillow at my face. Chuckling, I pull her in for a deep and breathless kiss.

Last night was out of this world. It felt like two souls made for each other finally coming together as one. For the last few months, I've been trying to hold my feelings back for Sorrel. But now I finally feel as free as a stallion running across the Montana mountain range. No one holding back my reins now.

I still need to tell her how I really feel. That I'm falling in love with her.

I look into her turquoise eyes. They're so full of hope and no longer full of trauma and fear. I brush loose locks of her white-blonde hair out of her face and marvel at her.

My phone starts buzzing from my pants that are still in a wet pile by the front door.

"Are you gonna get that?" she asks me.

"No, no way," I say going in for more kisses. We're both smiling into the kiss while we make out, our teeth clacking together, not even caring. I have a feeling whatever is on the other end of that phone is going to take away from this blissful high I'm on and I ain't willing to risk that for a damned thing right now.

But before I have the chance to stop her Sorrel pulls away from me, leaving me feeling un-whole again.

She grabs the pants and rummages around for my phone. "It's still ringing. Just answer it so we can go back to bed."

"If that's my prize, your wish is my command love."

Rolling her eyes and grinning wide, she hands me the phone. I look at it and cringe.

JAKE AGENT:

Missed call

Missed call

Missed call

5 iMessages

JOHNNY:

Denton what the fuck is going on?

GRADY:

Jake told us about the tour we got offered. Why didn't you tell us?

PARKER:

That's fucked up man.

JOHNNY:

Band meeting NOW! We're coming to get you Denton.

Fuck.

—

The next day I borrow Sorrel's Dodge Cummins to drive into town for our band meeting. I figured it'd be best to meet on neutral ground, back where we started this adventure. The boys were serious considering they hopped on the first flight out and got here this morning.

I enter into the hazy little bar and sit at the same table we sat at all those months ago. I haven't been back to the Wagon Wheel since the night Kenzington showed up and ruined it all.

We were having a blast up on that stage, and in a way, I felt at home up there. I could picture myself living at the ranch with Sorrel and coming into town every weekend to play here at the Wagon Wheel. Sorrel would be sitting at that table in the corner with Charli, watching us and sipping on their whiskeys. I'm sure the pay wouldn't be great, but we'd be having fun and I'd be happy. We could keep playing at rodeos too in the summer. No, it wouldn't be the big stage dreams we've always had but maybe it would be enough.

Is that what the other guys want though? Well, I guess I'm about to find out.

There they are—everyone except Ray—rolling in like a pack of pissed off hyenas. I can practically hear them growling. I'm smart enough to have four long necks sitting on the table ready for them. I hope it's enough to ease some of the tension.

They all sit down and I put my arms on the table ready to let them have at me.

"Well, have at it, y'all. Who wants to start?" I gesture to Johnny knowing it'd be him.

"You done playing cowboy yet, Denton?" Johnny asks.

I don't mean to, but I take up a defensive stance squaring my shoulders at him. "I'm not playing, Johnny. Never was."

"Yeah, sure," he says, crossing his arms.

"Why didn't you tell us about the tour?" Parker asks.

"I was going to. I meant to already. Things got crazy here at the ranch and then the fire happen—"

Johnny cuts in, talking over me. "Yeah, the fire Sorrel's crazy fucking ex started that almost cost us everything. What if your vocal cords had never healed Denton?"

"There are no what-ifs. They did heal and I can sing just fine," I say firmly.

Everyone is talking at once now and I can't hear myself think. Grady slams his fist on the table, bottles falling over and beer spilling. A stillness comes over everyone. Grady has always been the quiet one of the group but also the most level-headed.

"Look, everyone, it sounds like Denton has been through a lot. He didn't mean no harm and wasn't hiding anything from us purposefully. Right?"

"Right," I say back.

"So, tell us about the tour and where your head is at. We can work out the rest later," he finishes.

I start to explain how Jake called the second day we were at the ranch and that's when we got the offer. I didn't know at that time if it's what I wanted anymore. I wasn't sure I could still picture myself living that life—the fame, money, and everything else that comes with it. I know it wasn't fair to hide it from them. I tell them so.

Johnny looks like he wants to knock the stupid right out of me.

"Dent, this was always the plan and everything we've been working for. Don't let some chick get in your head and ruin it for us," he says.

My jaw clenches at the way he's talking about Sorrel and I need to think before I speak.

Very slowly I say to him, "This ain't about her, Johnny."

He rolls his eyes at me like he doesn't believe me. Do I really blame him though?

"If he says it's not, then I believe him," Parker says.

I nod in thanks to him.

Letting out a long deep breath, I put my face in my hands. How did this all get so fucked up?

"We're giving you until tomorrow, Denton, to make a decision. If we have to find a new lead singer, we will. This is what the rest of us want and nothing is going to get in our way," Johnny growls.

I unclench my fists and lay my hands flat on the table. "I understand. I'll let you know by tomorrow."

The bar is quiet now and I push my stool out

making a loud screeching sound. I bump my fist on the table and take them all in with genuineness

"I'm sorry, y'all."

None of them say a word.

Before I leave, I take in the bar one more time, staring at the stage. Imagining what might be a new dream forming in my heart. I have a lot of thinking to do on the drive back to the ranch.

My mind is a scrambled mess. Sorrel and I have just started something and how would it look if I just took off on a tour now? She would never forgive me for gaining her trust and then taking off. But she has to understand this isn't just about me and what I want. I have other people to think of here and this is about their livelihood. This tour would be life-changing for all of us.

I press my foot harder on the throttle. I have to get back to the ranch and get all of this off my chest.

Could I do another year on the road, chasing the dream that has consumed my life for so long? But then there's Sorrel. Strong, stubborn, and fiercely tied to this land that is nothing like the flashy world I know. The way Sutton looked at me this morning when she caught us together, the quiet support she offered us—it hit me hard. These women aren't just part of some story I would write about and turn into a song. They're my people now.

Can I really do this? Leave the tour behind or slow down? Could I live without the roar of the crowd and the adrenaline of the stage? And how could I ask Sorrel to share a piece of me when I barely know how to hold it myself. Hell, if there's even a piece left. Performing takes everything from me.

I grip the steering wheel harder winding around the mountain now that overlooks the Saxxon Ranch. I want to give Sorrel what she deserves—peace, safety, and a life worth holding on to. I could see it in her eyes—she believes in me, even if I'm not sure I deserve it.

Maybe there's a way—split the time, bring the tour closer to her, slow down enough to actually live. But the tour is calling—loud and relentless. Not figuratively but literally as I look down and see my agent Jake is calling again. I can't keep ignoring him. I answer this time.

"Hey, Jake, what's up?" I ask casually.

"Denton! What's up, man? Really? I've been trying to get a hold of you for weeks. I thought you went MIA at that dude ranch or something. Not fucking cool, man, that's what's up."

"It's not a dude ranch," I say flatly.

"Whatever you want to call it, I don't care. It's time to make a decision, Denton. Are you signing this contract or not?"

Fuck me. I thought I would have until tomorrow. I thought I'd be able to talk to Sorrel about this first. What the hell am I gonna do?

"Listen, the guys said I had until tomorrow and I need to talk to my girl—"

"No! None of that bullshit, Denton. Your girl? I don't give a shit about your girl. Decision needs to be made now."

I clear my throat, already dreading what comes out of my mouth next.

"Fine, we'll do it."

"That a boy—"

I cut him off before he can finish. "On one condition."

He lets out an exasperated breath. "Here we go. Fucking musicians. What is it?"

"I want to shift the tour venues to be in or near towns where there are pro rodeos. She's on the rodeo circuit, and if we're in the same town, when we're traveling, it'll work."

Jake chuckles. "You're serious? You want to plan a tour around a rodeo? This tour is nationwide. Do you really think she's gonna follow you all over the country?"

"Yeah, I am serious. This isn't just a fling, Jake. I want to make this work and this is the only way I think it will."

I can hear the reluctance in his voice.

"Fine. Just know I don't think it's a good idea and there better be no drama."

I let out a sigh of relief.

We talk logistics—dates, venues, and routes. The road won't be easy, but I'm determined to make this work with Sorrel. I hang up, feeling a weight lift off my shoulders and pull up the band group chat.

THE CREW

DENTON:

Tour is on.

. . .

As I pull up to the Saxxon Ranch, I stop in front of the gate. I sit here for a moment trying to find my bearings before driving in. A lump forms in the back of my throat and I'm nervous as hell to find out what Sorrel is going to think of all this.

20

SORREL

The sound of the dogs barking outside my cabin tell me Denton must be back from town. I'm so anxious to find out how the emergency band meeting went. I took the day off from ranch work but tried to stay busy while my mind raced with thoughts about me and Denton.

I cleaned the cabin and made us lunch to have outside on the porch in our usual spot. Walking out the front door, I feel my eyes crease from smiling—excited to jump into Denton's arms. But when he gets out of the truck, he has an uneasy look on his handsome face and my smile falters.

"Everything okay?" I ask from the top step—changing my mind about jumping into his arms.

He gives me a sheepish smile. "Oh yeah, everything's fine. What's that smell? Is that lunch? I'm starving," he says, changing the subject.

"Yeah, go ahead and sit down. I'll bring it out."

I made us green chili enchiladas. It's really the

only thing I know how to make that turns out good every time. It's Charli's recipe. Being from Texas, she makes the best Tex-Mex food—something we're desperately lacking in Montana.

I bring out two plates and forks, sit down next to Denton and hand him his plate. Dash is already at our feet begging.

Something is off and I'm no longer hungry but I do my best to eat anyway.

When we're both finished, I take our plates inside. Instead of leaving them in the sink, I set them on the floor to let Dash polish them off. I lean over the sink and let out a raspberry.

Marching back outside, I burst through the screen door. "Please tell me what's going on before I lose my damned mind, Denton."

"Come sit. It's kind of a lot."

I cross my arms, staying put. "No, I think I'd rather stand," I say.

I'd rather have my head held high and not be close to him when he tells me that he's leaving.

"Okay...it's about the tour," he says, stammering.

I already know I'm not going to like what he tells me next.

"So, we're going. We signed the contracts electronically and we're now obligated to a year-long, nationwide tour."

"Awesome. So happy for you." I spit out and turn on my heel to go back inside, but before I can, he jumps up and grabs my arm. "Sorrel, wait—"

"Let go, Denton," I say, looking down at my arm.

With sad eyes, he looks down at it too. "I'm sorry, Sorrel. Just please don't go before I'm finished giving you all the details."

I put my head up against the wall and hold myself, feeling my heart already breaking.

My voice hardens. "Fine, go on."

"I made a stipulation that they have to book us venues near any pro rodeos. We can travel together and both be on the road at the same time. Even if you only come for the summer. We would still be able to see each other and make this work."

He's planning his tour around pro rodeos, for me?

My heart stops and my mind is spinning.

"What are you even talking about, Denton? This isn't anything," I say, motioning between the two of us.

"C'mon now, Sorrel, you know that ain't true."

Is he really rearranging his whole tour just because of me? Does he really want us to be more? Something serious? My mind reels, taking it all in.

I want to believe him, but after everything with Huck…after all the lies and betrayal, trusting someone feels impossible.

I take off running toward the arena. I need to get away, to breathe, to think and be alone. I grab one of the saddled horses and jump on, taking off into a full run. When I turn around, he's standing there behind me with a look of hurt in his eyes as I take off leaving him in my dust.

• • •

I RIDE FAST AND HARD, PASSING A FEW HANDS MOVING some cattle, not paying them any attention.

Out of nowhere Sutton is on my tail.

"What the hell are you doing, Sorrel? Don't tell me you're running away from that boy already."

"Mind your business!" I yell back at her.

I'm tired of my nosy older sister. She doesn't understand. She doesn't know what I've been through.

She's on my flank now, damnit. Her horse Athena is faster than the old bay gelding I'm on.

"Just slow down, Sorrel. You're gonna give old grumps there a heart attack. He hasn't been ridden that hard in years."

I feel bad now. I should have made a better selection, but I picked the first horse I saw tied up. These horses are used for lessons or easy ranch work nowadays. I pull back on the reins slowing down to a smooth lope.

"Fine. Happy?"

"No, I still don't know what's going on with you."

We circle each other in the small clearing. I look around at the wildflowers sprouting—butterflies flutter in and out of the tall grass. I stop my horse and jump off, plopping down to the ground. Running my hands through the soft grass, I close my eyes and lift my face to the sun as my horse begins to graze—still holding the reins so he can't get too far away.

I lower my head to my knees and start crying. Sutton's off her horse now and she gently sits down next to me. Athena tries to graze but Sutton pulls her head up so she can't.

"Just let her graze," I say, sniffling.

"No, this is my good bit. I don't want her eating with it in her mouth."

Athena isn't giving up though, she's as stubborn as her owner. Sighing, Sutton lets her eat the grass she so desperately wants.

"So, tell me what's going on."

"It's Denton, as you already guessed."

"Well, what did he do? Do I need to have Ryder take him to the train station?" she says, referencing a thing from the show *Yellowstone*.

I let out a strained laugh and shake my head.

That show has made it so popular here in Montana. Everyone wants to be a cowboy now.

"He's going on tour. It's nationwide and he'll be gone for a whole year."

"Well, did he tell you that was a possibility before ya'll got together?"

"I mean kind of. He told me about it but said he wasn't sure if it was what he wanted anymore. But I guess now it is."

"Did he explain why?"

"I didn't really give him the chance."

I grimace thinking about how I just took off on him. "He said he's going to plan it around pro rodeos so I can travel with them or him with me. I'm not really sure what the hell he is thinking but there's no way that will ever work. I can't go rodeoing across the country. The ranch needs me, you guys need me—" She puts up a hand and stops me mid-sentence. "Sorrel, no offense, but we don't really need you."

"Wow, that's rude!" I say, shoving her shoulder.

She raises her brows and laughs.

"What? It's the truth. We have more than enough hands and you've always rodeoed most of the summer. You just haven't as much this year because you've been hiding from that douchebag."

"Yeah, I guess that's true. But I've always rodeoed here in Montana. Not across the country. It would be so much more in fuel and the cost of feed is higher in other states."

She narrows her eyes at me. "Sorrel, we can afford it. You're not getting any younger, and it's one summer. Hell, even if you traveled with them the whole year, it's not a long time. It sounds like a fun experience to me. I'd do it if I wasn't thirty and married with a child."

I start crying even more thinking about being away from Trotter. Missing out on seeing him grow for one whole year. Sutton knows exactly what I'm thinking before I say anything.

"Trotter will still be here. It's not like you can't come home at all. You know we would FaceTime you every night if that's what you want."

She's spot-on. I know she would. And I could come home if I wanted to. It's not like I'd be forced to stay on the road.

I look at her tears still rolling down my cheeks. "Thank you."

"You know, Sorrel, I've been through a lot with dating too. I'm always here for you. If you ever need advice, I've had my fair share of heartbreak. I just finally got smart enough to realize there was a good man in front of me all along."

"I know. I'm so happy for you and Ryder," I say, giving her hand a squeeze and she squeezes mine back. We hug and I wipe the tears from my face and brush the grass off the back of my pants. We both climb back into the saddle and I know I need to get back to my cabin to finish my conversation with Denton. If he's still there that is.

21

DENTON

My heart shattered in a million pieces when Sorrel ran away from me. I didn't know what to do next so I just waited. Part of me is frustrated with her for taking off and not letting me finish explaining everything. But I also understand why. She's scared. I thought she might react this way, but the lovesick cowboy in me imagined it going a little better than this.

It's been nearly an hour and she still isn't back. I'm beginning to worry that something might've happened to her.

Right as I'm about to go get Whiskey from the barn she comes trotting toward me on the back of a stocky bay gelding that looks like he's had some miles put on him. He's foamy from sweating and Sorrel's body is glistening with sweat too in the bright afternoon sunshine. Her bright blonde waves cascade down her back into a tangled knot from not braiding it before taking off on her wild ride. Her eyes are puffy and red. She wipes at her nose on the sleeve of her T-shirt as she trots closer to me.

I approach her slowly like a stray dog that might take off if you get too close too fast.

She dismounts the bay horse and I reach to take the reins from her. She lets me have them, but she doesn't look me in the eyes.

"I'll put him up for you."

"Thanks… I—I'm sorry, Denton. I shouldn't have taken off like that."

"No, you shouldn't have," I tell her.

She looks back at me, her lips turned down. I can understand her pain, her trauma, and having a guard up. I've been patient with her and let her work through all of it but I'm not a damned doormat she can walk all over.

She clears her throat. "Ever since you got to this ranch, I've been pushing you away and you've been nothing but patient and kind. More than anything you've been a good friend to me, Denton. You deserve more than I can give you."

"No."

"No?"

"No," I say more sternly since she isn't getting it.

"What do you mean no?"

"I mean no, you don't get to pull that shit. You are enough for me, Sorrel. You're more than I've ever dreamed of and I'm not letting you run away anymore. You're gonna face it," I say, pointing at her heart. "Face what you feel in there."

Tears start to form in her eyes and she just nods

and reaches for me. I take her into my arms and just hold her. I let her get it all out not caring that my gray T-shirt is soaked through with her tears.

If this is who she needs, I'll be that person for her. If she needs me to be firm with her, I will. No more holding back for either of us.

"Sorrel," I say softly, brushing her hair out of her face and wiping away her tears.

"I love you damnit," I tell her, chuckling. A rush of relief surges through me for finally saying it.

"You do?" she squeaks.

"I'm still here, aren't I?"

"You're still here," she says, holding me tighter as if she's making sure all of this is real.

I swoop her into my arms and point us in the direction of her cabin. She presses her mouth against mine, pulling my head in closer like she can't get enough of my mouth on hers. I stumble up the stairs trying not to fall, but there's no way I'm breaking contact with her right now.

We make it through the door, both of us panting and I head for her bedroom. I lay her down roughly on the bed and she gently tugs at the bottom of my curls. I can tell she wants more of me this time—rougher. I'm not worried like last time; her body is telling me everything I need to know.

"Off," is all she says, gesturing to her jeans.

I do as she commands, undoing the button and then the zipper ripping her skin-tight jeans off her long tan legs. For being a cowgirl, she somehow has a great tan and her legs are tone from hours in the saddle every day.

She surprises me when she flips me over and climbs on top of me. I'm more than happy to be the bronc she rides today. Her breathing is heavy and hurried. She's so fucking sexy.

She moves faster and faster and I can't hold it back any longer and we both come apart together. She flops down lying next to me, a lazy smile on her face. Her smile is contagious and I flash an identical one back at her. Everything about this moment is pure bliss and I don't want to ruin it by bringing up the tour again but we have to finish our conversation.

"So, you won't run away again when we talk about the tour, right?"

"No, that was stupid of me and I'm sorry, Denton."

She lays her head on my chest now.

"I don't want to keep doing that. I know it's something I need to work on. I've always avoided confrontation and anytime I've had it in a relationship I automatically assumed it meant it was over. With Huck that's always how it was—fight equals breakup. I see it's a fucked-up pattern now."

I tilt her face to look up at me.

"We're gonna fight sometimes, Sorrel, that's just part of it. But I need you to know, just because we don't agree on something doesn't mean I'm gonna walk away."

"God, I love how emotionally mature you are. It's so hot."

I laugh at that. "Well, I've got a few years on you and a little more life experience."

"Oh yeah, old man?" she says, winking at me.

"Yeah, darlin', I was on this earth for four years before you ever were. I learned a thing or two in my day."

"Oh whatever. I'm about to be twenty-six and you're twenty-nine. It's not that big of a difference."

"Just admit I, Denton Reed, know more than you, Sorrel Saxxon."

"Never!" she says with a wicked grin as she creeps over, trying to tickle me.

We roll and wrestle and eventually start making out again, which leads to more mind-blowing love-making. I'm so in love with this wild cowgirl. I think she might be the one for me.

22

SORREL

After we make love for the third time that afternoon, we're finally ready to finish our conversation about the tour. Denton explains to me how he told his agent Jake he would only agree to sign the contract if the venues are in or near towns that have pro rodeos.

"So, you really told him you would only do the tour if we could travel together?"

"Yeah, I did. He wasn't happy about it, but I don't give a flying fuck. I'm doing my best to make everyone happy, but you're a priority for me now, Sorrel. I hope you know that."

God, this man can't be real. I don't know what I did to deserve him. I'm so smitten with him it's sickening.

"I know that, Denton. You are for me too. I just don't want to be a burden to you when we're on the road."

I want to make sure he feels my support, and that

he doesn't ever feel like he's babysitting me while trying to be a rockstar.

He rolls his eyes. "Sorrel, you could never be a burden. You're everything to me."

I melt into him, at a loss for words. How does he always know the right thing to say to me?

I know life on the road probably won't be as glamorous as it seems and there will undoubtedly be a lot of times when we won't be able to see each other. But I believe him when he says he'll do anything to make this work.

We're both starving now after everything, so I heat us up some of the green chili enchiladas while Denton starts us a fire. He makes us a cozy spot on the floor in front of the fireplace with lots of blankets and pillows. It's adorable and Dash is already burrowed under one of the blankets.

We sit down with our food and all we can see is Dash's little nose sticking out from under the blanket sniffing at our food. We both laugh and it makes my heart happy that he loves my little dog. Most cowboys act all tough and hate on barrel racers having little sausage dogs. Not Denton though. He loves all dogs. His heart is so big and it makes me fall for him even more.

I still haven't said "I love you" back but it doesn't seem to bother him. I know I'm falling in love with him but I'm just not ready to say it yet. Maybe a good lecture from Charli will give me some courage. I make a mental note to give her a call tomorrow morning.

"Hey, I have an idea," I tell Denton, sitting up straighter with excitement.

"Oh yeah, what's that?" he asks, shoveling in another mouthful of enchiladas.

"A concert. Here, tonight. We have new guests for the week. I bet they would love a free Denton Reed concert. Might get us a big tip," I say, wagging my brows.

"Wha–what about my stuff?" he asks, shooting up and looking toward the guesthouse.

"Oh yeah, I meant to tell you when you got back today, but I figured you could just stay with me now. It doesn't feel right to keep charging you and I added you onto the payroll for the time being. Lucy brought your stuff over while you were gone this morning. I guess you didn't notice it in the corner of my room." I point toward his belongings, snickering.

"No, I was a little distracted, wasn't I?" he says, giving me a wink.

"Well, what do you think? We can make a makeshift stage and everything with some wood pallets."

"All right I'm in. You don't have to twist my arm to get me to do a little singing."

He has some enchiladas in the corner of his mouth and it makes me giggle. His light green eyes are sparkling, dimple showing, and I think he's truly happy here.

One year on the road, we'll get through, it and then maybe I can talk him into a year here in

Montana after that or at least a full summer. I'm not sure what the future has in store for us but I can't wait to find out. After all these months full of drama with Huck, denying my feelings for Denton, and then almost dying in a fire, I finally feel like everything is going to be okay. Like my life isn't some great big pile of cow shit I keep stepping in. No, it feels good—hell better than good. I'm finally figuring out who I truly am and the type of person I want to be. Part of that is because of Denton. When you're with the right person, a lot can change and for the better.

. . .

Our new guests are having supper with us, and their teenage daughter about fainted when she saw Denton sitting at the table. We all held back our laughs, not wanting to embarrass her.

Her name is Sofia. She's only thirteen and still growing into her long skinny legs. She has dark brown hair and beautiful sun-kissed skin which I assume she got from living in the Arizona desert. She barrel races too and her face lit up when Sutton told her that I'm a professional barrel racer. She asked if I could help her on her first barrel. She's been blowing past it during her runs. I of course told her I would give her some pointers tomorrow morning. I'll put her on Duke. I trust him with any level rider.

The whole family is sweet as can be. Her dad doesn't ride at all and her mom rode when she was a kid. Her younger brother rides dirt bikes, and Denton and him talk about the different types of bikes and racing throughout dinner. Apparently, Denton used to race dirt bikes too. I have to admit, there's still so much I don't know about him. I'm looking forward to learning more about this man when we travel together. I could sit here and watch him all night. The way he interacts with the guests and the genuine smile and care he gives them stirs something inside of me. He's so good with people and I know he's meant to be famous, to make a difference in people's lives—even if it's only for a short moment.

He's talking with Sofia now, asking her about school and barrel racing. She keeps brushing a stray lock of hair behind her ear every few seconds. It's cute how nervous she is around him and I don't blame the girl. I still feel the same way sometimes. She asks if she can take a selfie with him and of course he says yes. It's not totally weird to see—well, maybe a little weird to see at our dinner table—but it reminds me of the fact that this is part of his life. There won't be any more hiding from it in a few short weeks. I just hope I can handle all the attention and women throwing themselves at him when we're on the road. I was never the jealous type before Huck, but his cheating brought out insecurities I never knew I had. I tried to bury them but clearly that wasn't working. The mature thing to do would be to talk with Denton about them before we leave. But part of me feels myself crawling back into that hole I buried everything in. I push the thought away for later and bring myself back to the present.

Everyone is getting up from their seats now, finished with another delicious dinner made by Jo.

"Any way we can take that cook home to Arizona with us?" Sofia's dad asks jokingly, but I think he might actually be serious. He had three heaping piles of Jo's famous cowboy casserole. It's a mouthwatering mixture of tater tots, ground beef, pinto beans, black beans, sour cream, and *lots* of cheese. Yum.

"Not a chance, but I'm sure she'd give you the recipe for her cowboy casserole," Dad tells him as they walk out onto the porch and the rest of us follow behind.

I cover my ears when Sofia lets out a high-pitched-scream. Her body exuberates with excitement as she jumps up and down when she sees the stage the ranch hands set up for our little concert tonight.

I look at Denton, and he just laughs. "You'll get used to the fan girl scream," he says.

"I highly doubt that," I respond, laughing nervously.

Crease is striding over to me and Denton now, guitar case in hand. He nearly trips over his long gangly legs when he sees Sofia. Denton and I both chuckle under our breath, trying to hold back our smiles.

Recovering and brushing himself off, Crease hands Denton his guitar. "Sorrel said you needed this."

"Yeah, thanks, Crease. Let me introduce you to someone," Denton says, leading him to where Sofia is standing by the front of the makeshift stage. I can see the blush on Crease's cheeks from a mile away. Oh, to be young again. My mind flashes back to the night I met Denton and I think my cheeks probably looked a little something like that.

I smile softly to myself replaying the night we met in my head as I walk over to the cooler set up with beer and hard seltzers. The ranch hands are all crowded around it now, and from deep within the group, I hear a voice with a sweet southern tang. I'd know that voice anywhere.

"Charli?" I call out, unable to see her surrounded by the group of cowboys whom most are over six feet tall. She shoves through them to get to me, beer in her hand and an unlit cigarette in the other.

"There she is!" Throwing her arm over my shoulder, she hands me her beer. I take a swig and it's already warm and flat.

"How long have you been here for?"

"Damn near an hour. Clint invited me since you're too busy with your new *boyfriend* for me now," she says, puckering her lower lip and making a sad face.

I groan and feel terrible for how little time I've had for her lately. I need to thank Dad later for inviting her tonight.

"If I break into Dad's liquor cabinet and get the good stuff, will it make up for it?" I ask, giving her big puppy-dog eyes.

She sighs. "You know, I can't stay mad at you, Sorrel Saxxon. Especially if you're offering me some Johnnie Walker Blue."

I link her arm in mine and look back making sure Dad is distracted before sneaking into his stash.

Johnnie Walker Blue is Dad's favorite scotch. It's expensive so he only ever drinks it on special occasions. I grab us two red Solo cups and twist the top off the bottle, pouring the brown liquor into our cups. Dad will make us both shovel horse shit with a fork for weeks if he catches us, especially for drinking it out of plastic cups.

We both giggle like schoolgirls as I hurry up and put the bottle back. It feels like we're in high school all over again. Except in high school, we knew better and went for the cheap vodka, replacing it with water. We were grounded for a month when Dad poured one of his buddies' wives a drink and she said it didn't taste like it had any liquor in it.

"Boots up, whiskey down!" we say as we cheers.

We make our way back outside and head toward the fire. The bonfire is roaring now, bright orange and red pieces of ash fluttering down landing in our hair. Everyone is huddled around talking and sipping on their drinks while Denton and "his band" get ready to perform. His band for tonight is just him and one of the ranch hands named Walker who plays guitar and can hum a little tune.

Everyone gathers around the stage now. Sofia right up front and Crease at her heels. The rest of her family stay seated by the fire facing their chairs to the stage. They aren't used to the cool bite of Montana summer nights. Summer is almost over and temperatures are dropping as fast as the flies.

Denton and Walker begin to play. A look of confusion spreads across my face—trying to recognize the song. It must be a new one and it seems like Walker is familiar with it.

Denton sings about a fierce cowgirl with demons in her mind, and she struggles to overcome her grief. I know he wrote the song about me. I turn away as tears begin to well in my eyes, wiping them away before anyone notices. But Charli already does.

"It's beautiful," she says.

I nod, tears now streaming down my face. God, I'm getting tired of crying all the damn time. But these aren't sad tears, not really.

Charli gives me a hug. "I can't believe my best friend is gonna marry a famous country music singer. That is so fucking rad."

I almost puke up the scotch when she mentions marriage.

"We are not getting married, Charli. That's not even funny."

"No, it's not funny. It's fucking *romantic.*"

Rolling my eyes at her and not giving this conversation another minute, I go to get another drink. One seltzer, two beers, and three shots later, it hits me.

Everyone is singing and dancing now and I'm sitting here drunk by myself while my boy—no, not my boyfriend, my friend—continues to perform for everyone. I look around me and see how happy everyone is. Sutton and Ryder are dancing with Trotter. He's shaking his little booty and his big ol' cowboy hat flops all over his head. Damn I'm going to miss this. It makes me realize what I'm missing out on even when I'm gone rodeoing. No, not every night is like this but a lot of them are.

Lost in my thoughts, I look up to see Charli surrounded by three of the younger ranch hands. I stumble over to them to try and save her but trip on some loose gravel. Just as I start to fall, two lean muscular arms catch me.

"Are you my knight in shining armor?" I say, looking up to see Denton's intense eyes staring back at me. "You are!" I giggle and hiccup, reaching for the scruff on his face. It feels good underneath my hand and I wonder what it would feel like in other places.

"I think you better get little miss rodeo queen to bed now," Charli says to Denton.

"Yeah, I think you're right," he says, looking at me, probably wondering how I got to be such a drunken mess.

"Hey, I'm not a rodeo queen. I'm a damn barrel racer!" I spit out.

The ranch hands are all laughing at me now. It sobers me up a little bit. I don't want word getting back to Dad that they saw me like this.

I grab Denton's hand and drag him toward my cabin. "Let's go."

Before we leave, he turns to Charli. "You gonna be okay with them alone, Charli?"

The ranch hands turn their rough faces to Denton giving him a dirty look.

"I'll be fine. Thanks for asking. I'll just sleep in my old room at Clint's. You'll take care of her, right?"

"Of course. I've got her, Charli."

"Awwww, I love you guys"—*hiccup*—"you're my best friends." I spread my arms wide and pull them in for a group hug.

Denton swoops me into his arms and carries me to the cabin.

"Wait. Put me down before we go through the door."

"Why?"

"Because you're not carrying me over a threshold until we get married. It's bad luck."

"Oh, is that right?" he asks with a smirk. "And when are we getting married?"

"Who knows?" I say with a drunken sigh.

When we get into the cabin, I stand by the front door, holding on to the frame while Denton pulls off my boots for me. I walk to the bedroom and strip out of my clothes as I go. I watch Denton follow the trail of clothing I left on the floor to the bed. I lay here waiting for him in just my bra and panties.

"Sorrel, I love you and you look sexy as hell right now, but you're drunk as a damn skunk. We're going to bed."

I look at him and frown, tracing circles with my fingertips on the mattress. I watch him get out of his clothes and admire every muscle and flex of his body. He's a fucking masterpiece.

My eyelids begin to get heavy and the room starts to spin. Mixing alcohol will do that to a girl. I wait for the spinning to stop and feel him crawl in under the covers next to me. He covers me up and kisses the top of my forehead before we both drift into a restless and needy sleep.

23

DENTON

I wake up to Sorrel softly breathing in my ear. Even in her sleep her natural beauty is astounding. Her blonde waves are scattered in every which way and her eyelids flutter like she must be dreaming about something.

I have a feeling she isn't going to be feeling her best today so I go in search of some Advil for the pounding headache I assume she'll have when she wakes up. It's tucked away in her medicine cabinet and I shake a few out in my hand to leave by her bedside with a glass of water.

There's no way we'll make it in time for breakfast at the main house so I scour through the fridge to see what I can throw together. There are eggs, some bread and cheese. Eggs sandwiches it is then. Dash is pawing at his food bowl, demanding his breakfast be served now. I fill up his bowl and give him a little pat on the head while he eats like it's his last meal on earth. Laughing, I begin working on the sandwiches.

Eggs over medium with melted cheese on top and toasted bread. Hopefully it will be edible. My mom taught me to cook when I was younger but tour life is mostly fast food or the occasional steak at a restaurant. Maybe we could steal Jo away to come on tour with us and cook all our meals. Clint would probably lock her away in hiding if we even suggested it. I hear a groan come from the bedroom.

"My head hurts," she calls out.

"Advil on the nightstand," I holler back to her.

When she emerges from the dark room, she's covering her eyes and squinting.

"Too bright out here."

I'm trying to hold back my laughter. She was hilarious last night. The way she talked about marriage, I kind of hope her drunken thoughts are her sober truths.

"Breakfast is ready. Sit down," I tell her, motioning to the round wooden table in the corner of the kitchen. I place the plate down in front of her and she makes a gagging noise as she tries to take a bite.

I almost spit my food out laughing. "That bad, huh?"

"No, I'm sorry. It's just the smell of the eggs." She plugs her nose, trying again.

"It's really good," she mumbles with food in her mouth and her nose plugged.

I've never seen her like this and it's cute to see her not all put together for once. She takes a few more bites and then gives the rest to Dash. I finish mine off and clear our plates.

"So," I say, over my shoulder as I wash the plates in the sink.

"The tour is approaching fast and I'm going over dates with Jake and the guys on a Zoom call today."

I look back over my shoulder to see she's not looking at me. She's in a daze staring out the open front door.

"Okay, sounds good," is all she says, when she finally replies. It seems like her head is in a totally different place.

"Did you want to be a part of it or listen in?"

"Um no, I think I'm good. I decided for the fall shows I'll probably just ride along with you guys if that's okay. Then in the summer is when I'll bring my rig and rodeo."

My eyes light up. I get excited she'll be on the road with us and really get to take it all in for the first part of the tour.

"Sounds great! So, uh, do remember what you said last night?"

She cringes and looks down at her ballerina-pink nails.

"Not much," she admits.

Finished with the dishes, I go up behind her and give her a shoulder rub. She moans with pleasure and it sends a shock through my core. I glance down at my phone and realize it's already past eleven. Fuck I wish I had more time before the Zoom meeting to carry her back to bed and give her what she wanted last night.

"My meeting starts soon. Why don't you go sleep

off your hangover a little more? I'll take the meeting on the porch so I don't disturb you."

"You're too good to me," she says with a soft smile. Tilting her chin up toward me, I lean down and give her a warm and gentle kiss.

She walks back to the bedroom and Dash takes off after her, losing traction on the hardwood floor, trying to keep his long body straight.

"Chill, little dude, she's not leaving you." I laugh.

Shit, it's 11:10 a.m. and the meeting is in five minutes. I grab my laptop and a glass of sweet tea and get comfortable in my rocking chair on the porch. I like the fact that I now have my own designated rocking chair. It's really starting to feel like home here.

I know Sorrel and I will both miss our lives here at the ranch and our afternoon lunches we spend together on the porch swing. I can picture living a slow life here with her, but I committed to at least one year of touring and we'll make new memories together on the road.

If there's one way to test a relationship, it's traveling together. The stress of driving and being in different towns with sleepless nights started to wear on me when I was single.

It'll be interesting to see how I'll handle it now with another person. A person whose feelings I care about.

The Zoom call connects and the guys are all here. Even Ray—it's important he gets all the details and dates of the tour too. Jake jumps right into it.

We now have a tour manager. Her name is Emily.

She seems nice enough but I'm not sure how good she'll fit in with me and the guys. I'll make sure we all at least give her a chance. We start the tour off on September third, in Knoxville, Tennessee, and from there we travel around the United States with three shows on and three to four days off in between. We'll be on the road until November fifth and then we break until the new year.

My stomach is starting to hurt and my nerves are on edge. It's a lot to take in. There are more performances than I realized there would be. I've gotten way too settled in here at the ranch and I feel like my whole world is about to be turned upside down.

. . .

Later that afternoon Sorrel helps Sofia with her first barrel. She missed their lesson this morning due to her hangover but she's feeling better now. I sit on the arena fence watching them. She's a great teacher and so patient with her, really taking her time to explain everything. I imagine her teaching a little cowgirl of her own how to barrel race someday. She'll be an amazing mother. My mind wanders and thinking about her bred makes the zipper of my pants twitch. I've never thought about anyone this way and there's so many feelings stirring in me I feel like I'm going to burst with happiness.

After their lesson we have dinner in the main house with everyone. When I finally get her alone, it takes everything in me not to grab her and rip her clothes off. She finally puts me out of my misery and we practice that breeding part I was thinking about earlier.

SEPTEMBER IS HERE BEFORE WE KNOW IT. THE LAST few weeks on the ranch have been nothing short of heavenly. I spent most of my days helping Ryder with ranch work. We fixed fences, worked on equipment, and made sure we have enough hay and grain for the Montana winter. Sorrel harvested the rest of her garden before everything died from the cold. I loved seeing her out there covered in dirt and squealing with excitement when she finally got a normal-looking carrot. She had started the garden over the summer as a new hobby when she quit rodeoing for that brief time. Her garden flourished just like she had. When I met her earlier in the year, I knew something inside of her was broken. But now she's healing and reclaiming her wholeness. It hasn't been easy but I'm damn sure glad to be part of her journey.

We leave tomorrow morning and I want to ask her to officially be my girlfriend.

"So, you gonna tell me where we're going? I'm not sure how safe being blindfolded on horseback is," Sorrel says.

"I've got you, darlin', don't you know that by now?"

I put her on Duke and I have him ponying next to Whiskey so I can surprise her. I probably shouldn't have rode Whiskey because she keeps pinning her ears and nipping at Duke every few feet.

"Quit being a bitch," I tell her as I pull her head away from him.

"Well, that was *rude*!" Sorrel laughs.

"Not you—the damn horse!"

"You really know how to woo a girl, Reed," she deadpans.

I'm fucking this all up. I want it to be perfect. The sound of cascading water now surrounds us, and I'm sure she's probably figured out where I've taken her. A grin tugs at her lips as I go to take off her blindfold.

24

SORREL

When Denton takes the blindfold off, a smile spreads across my face. He has a blanket set up on the grassy bank by the water. His guitar is sitting next to a small cooler on the blanket.

So that's what he was doing when he snuck off earlier.

He thought I didn't see him when I had my head buried in my garden, but out of the corner of my eye, I saw him on horseback with his guitar strapped to him and cooler in one hand. I didn't want to spoil his surprise so I kept it to myself.

He takes my hand, leading me over. He seems all flustered and I can't help but snicker at him.

"What's all this for?" I ask as we sit down and I fold my legs under me.

Here he goes again making me feel like a kid and all giddy inside.

"I wrote you another song. It just sorta came to

me one night and I couldn't wait any longer to sing it to you." He blushes

I fan my forehead and fake faint as I swoon at him. He laughs.

"I told you before. You're my muse. I'm in love and I can't help it."

His eyes, drop a shade deeper, and he takes my face in his big hands and brushes his soft lips against mine, teasing me. I close the gap and kiss him. A deep hungry kiss. My core aches and throbs for him. I reach for his shirt and tear it open, unfastening the pearl snaps—revealing his smooth chiseled chest. He pulls the tank top over my head; the cool air makes the skin on my chest prickle.

I have to have him now. We both work at each other's pants and they're off in seconds. Denton lifts me up off the ground and I let out a surprise yelp before he softly lowers me on my back. He takes me in, admiring my body like it's the first time all over again.

"Fuck, Sorrel, you have me speechless and you know damn well that's a rarity for me."

I give him my best seductive grin and pull him down onto me. I run my hands through his soft curls and tilt my head back listening to the sound of the water rippling. Once we've thoroughly gotten enough of each other we dip off in the creek and then sun our naked bodies until we're dry.

Denton cracks us each open a beer while we lie there and attempt to fix our farmers' tans. We put our clothes back on and I lie out on the blanket, staring up at him while he finally sings me the song he wrote for me.

It's called "Everything He Didn't Do." I choke back tears as he sings.

"I know he hurt you, just give me one shot to pick up where he left off, ' cause you deserve more than that. Yeah, you deserve better, you deserve forever. Baby, give me one shot, he put you through the ringer, damn sure won't put a ring on your finger, but you deserve forever, so let me do everything he didn't do…"

"You deserve the world, Sorrel," he says, when he finishes singing.

I'm momentarily struck speechless as I sniffle and smile, unable to find the right words to say.

"Sorrel, you already know I'm in love with you. Before we leave on this tour, I want to ask you if you'll do me the honor and officially be my girlfriend?"

He falters when I don't immediately respond, his face turning into a frown.

"I love you too," I say as I press my mouth against his

He perks up in surprise. While my mouth is pushed against his, he mumbles, "And what about the girlfriend part?"

I laugh. "Yes, yes, of course I will, Denton."

My heart swells and I can't be any happier than I am in this moment right now. Tomorrow, we leave for the tour and I'll be Denton Reed's fucking girlfriend. I didn't expect to have that on my bingo card this year.

When summer started, I was a broken fucking

mess. Huck hurt me in so many ways. I wasn't sure I would ever move past it. I'll never forget what he did to me but I can see now what a good man really is. My walls were up and I had no room for love in my heart when I met Denton. I never in a million years would have thought someone like him would be a good and loving man. But I judged who he was and assumed that all cowboys are the same. I was so wrong. And I'm happy to say so.

I feel more confident than ever now to go on tour with Denton. I'll miss my family and the ranch but I'm excited for this adventure to come.

. . .

Our last night at the ranch is of course filled with family time and one of Jo's specials. She made us a large roast with mashed potatoes, carrots, and gravy. My mouth is watering and my stomach is grumbling. Denton and I sure worked up an appetite this afternoon. When we walked into everyone already seated at the table, they stared at us like they knew what we'd been up to all afternoon. Well, everyone except Dad. He's always oblivious to it all—probably on purpose. He likes Denton but he doesn't ever get too involved. As long as us girls are happy that's all that matters to him.

After we're done with the main course, Jo brings out my favorite, brownies and ice cream. Trotter has finished his and moved onto mine as he sits in my lap and I share with him. Chocolate covers his mouth and little round cheeks. His fingers are sticky and covered in ice cream. I laugh as I try to dodge him from putting them on my face. Dash jumps up, paws on my thigh, and laps the ice cream off his hands. Trotter breaks into a fit of laughter. My cheeks hurt from smiling so much. I'll be counting down the days until I'm back at this table with my family again. I love them so much it hurts. But that love is growing and a sweet cowboy has squeezed his way into the tiny space that was left in my heart.

—

Morning comes quickly and I wake before Denton. Dash and I quietly sneak out of the cabin to go watch the sunrise.

The chill of the cool morning breeze hits my face as I wrap my blanket around me tighter. I sit on the porch swing, Dash in my lap. The sun begins to rise behind the mountains—a true masterpiece. Fiery red and orange clouds scatter the sky as a curtain of light lay over the green valley below. A brood mare and her baby trot through the pasture coming in to be fed.

Denton joins me—I must not have been as quiet as I thought. He wraps his long arms around me—right where I'm meant to be. I settle in resting my head on his chest. We swing back and forth without saying a word, just admiring the view. When I'm old and gray this is where I'll go—the memories I'll look back on. Just me and him here in the quiet. No work, no worries—just us and this land.

. . .

We finish packing, and I tidy up my cabin so there won't be much for Lucy to clean. I'm getting Dash's bowls and food when I hear the thundering engine of the tour bus. Denton goes out to greet the guys and I step out on the porch just watching for a moment.

It's strange to see the bus here again. It's almost like they never left. Ray starts loading our bags up. He goes to grab mine from my hands. "I got it," I say to him.

"Now, Miss Sorrel, don't be putting me out of a job. I'll be taking care of your bags for you as long as you're on my bus."

No point in arguing, I guess. I let him take the bags from me. I'll need some kind of job myself. There's no way I'll make it through the next few months without something to keep me busy.

"Welcome to the band, Sorrel!" Johnny teases.

I scoff. "You don't want me in the band, trust me. I don't have a musical bone in my body."

"Well, that's gonna have to change. You're dating a musician now."

I laugh. That's not happening.

I'm ready to get on the road before I chicken out. There will be three days of driving before the first concert in Knoxville, Tennessee.

Ryder and Sutton ride up on their horses, here to

give us their farewells. Dad and Trotter come out of the main house.

"No!" Trotter screams, running away from Dad.

He's running so fast his little head smacks into the top of my knee before I can catch him. Trotter wails, rubbing at his head. I pick him up into my arms.

"I love you so much, baby. We won't be gone long."

"Don't go!" he whines, and stretches his arms out toward Denton.

"He wants you," I say, handing him to Denton.

He whispers something in Trotter's ear and he immediately stops crying. A playful smile now spreads across his little lips.

"What'd you promise him?" Sutton asks, climbing down from her horse. Ryder doesn't get off his.

Grinning, Denton says, "That Auntie Sorrel and I will bring him home lots of presents and treats."

Sutton rolls her eyes and is biting back a smile.

She takes Trotter from his arms and sits him atop her horse—he is happy as can be now, horseback. She gives us both hugs, saying her goodbyes and Ryder shakes Denton's hand. I just give him a smile and wave. He isn't really the touchy feely type and gets weird when it comes to goodbyes.

Last to say goodbye is Dad. He takes me in and I breathe in his scent. He smells of leather and the cologne he wears every day. It's a musky warm scent. I hope I'll always remember his smell.

"I love you, darlin'. You be safe out there, and if you need to come home, give me a call. We'll get you a flight, bus, one of them Guber things, whatever we gotta do."

I laugh. "I know, Dad. I love you too."

It's time now; Denton and I lock hands. The guys all give him shit. I expect there will be a lot of that—boys will be boys.

Next stop, Knoxville, Tennessee.

25

DENTON

We've been on the road for three days. Sorrel is fitting in great with the guys, giving them just as much shit as they give her. Johnny has actually met his match. He keeps asking her to FaceTime Charli, and every time she does, she ends up giving him her phone and they talk for hours. I think there might be something there. They already talked about flying her out to a few shows. Dash has settled into being a road dog and spends most of his time sleeping in the bed we put underneath the dinette booth.

We're almost to the venue now and I'm feeling a little tense. We are about to perform in front of thousands of people and I haven't been up in front of a crowd in a while. I was quiet today, and if Sorrel could tell, she didn't say so but hopefully she understands it's just nerves.

"How are you feeling about tonight?" she asks me

as I turn my attention away from staring out the window.

We're sitting at the dinette booth and I don't think I've said a word for almost an hour.

"He always gets off beat before a big show, Sorrel. Don't take it personal," Parker tells her.

She gives him a tight smile and looks back to me expectantly.

"He's right. It's just nerves. I'll be fine once I'm up there."

"No problem, I get it," she says sincerely. "I always get nervous before a big rodeo. If there's anything I can do to help, I'll be here, but if you need time to yourself, that's cool too."

"Thanks, baby."

She smiles back and opens one of the seven new books she bought at a local bookstore when we were driving through Kentucky. She's excited to finally have time to read so I leave her to it. I stand up, then lean over and give her a kiss.

I walk to the front of the bus to go sit in the front seat by Ray. He isn't much for words and I know I can just close my eyes and meditate while I'm up here.

. . .

We arrived at the Thompson-Boling Arena a few hours ago. Mentally I feel rested and much better now that we're here. We went through sound check and rehearsal. Now it's time to get ready and hangout for a while before the show.

Sorrel comes out from the bathroom and my jaw drops to the floor. She has a little more makeup on than usual and curled her hair. Her short denim skirt shows off her long sleek legs and she has on a pair of boots I haven't seen her wear before. She bends over looking for her cowboy hat in one of the cabinets and I can see down her tank top. I instantly feel turned on. Man, this is going to be more distracting than I thought.

She plops her cowboy hat on her head. "I'm ready. Bathroom's free." she calls out to all of us.

We all let her get ready first. Johnny lets out a whistle and I glare at him in return.

"You look awesome, babe." I reach for her hips and pull her into me.

"No PDA on the bus," Parker says, handing Sorrel the drink he poured for her.

She takes it and thanks him before taking a sip.

"Woo, that's strong!" She cringes down at the cup.

I chuckle. "I should have warned you. Don't let Parker make you a drink. He's got a heavy pour."

"Clearly," she states. "You gonna go get ready?"

"Yeah, I'll see you in a bit." I kiss her on the cheek instead of the mouth not wanting to get anymore turned on than I already am. I can't be up on stage with a hard-on all damn night.

When I come out from showering and getting dressed, there's a new face on the bus. She looks me up and down like I'm a tasty sirloin steak she's about to devour.

I look around at the guys with confusion like, *Who the fuck is this and what did you do with my girlfriend?*

The mystery woman gets up and strides over to me. She's about average height with a short brown bob, dark brown eyes, and an alluring smile.

"I'm Emily, your tour manager," she says, putting out her hand to shake mine. I shake hers back. She holds onto my hand for a beat too long as I try to pull it away.

"Denton," is all I say to her. I look past her at the crew. "Where's Sorrel?"

"Oh, I asked her to step out so we could go over some things. I know boys will be boys, but I suggest no groupies on the bus before showtime."

I don't even respond. Storming past her, I walk out of the bus to go find my girlfriend. The sun is setting now and Sorrel is nowhere to be found.

"SORREL!" I call out to her.

"I'm over here."

I hear her small voice come out from behind the bus. It looks like she's hanging up a call.

"Get back in here," I insist.

"Miss Lady said you guys needed to go over things alone."

"Yeah, well Miss Lady don't know what the fuck she's talking about."

She follows me inside without arguing, Dash trotting along next to us.

"Emily, this is my *girlfriend*, Sorrel Saxxon."

Dash is growling at her and Emily scowls looking down at him.

"We met," she says flatly, turning back to Grady.

"So anyways, do you boys have everything you need? I have the set list here. Denton, let's go over it."

My fists clench and I reach into my pocket to pull out my phone.

DENTON:

We need a new tour manager ASAP!

JAKE:

I'll try but you'll have to stick with her for the next few shows.

DENTON:

Fine.

I take Sorrel's hand and lead her to the open lounge seat gesturing for her to sit. She raises an eyebrow and I pull her down into the seat sitting next to her on the arm of the chair.

Emily glances up at her rolling her eyes just long enough for me to catch her. I swear if she tries to run Sorrel off, she's going to see a side of me that doesn't come out very often.

I let out a deep breath. I don't need this bullshit right before the show. I'll let it go for tonight. But there is no way this is going to work for the whole tour.

The tour manager's job is to travel with us and make sure everything is going correctly. I'm not about to have some stuckup broad be our tour manager that won't be respectful to my girl.

We go over the set list and there's one hour until the show starts. Everything is ready to go.

I pour myself a drink. My choice of liquor tonight is vodka. Hopefully it will settle my nerves and numb me enough I don't keep getting turned on every time I look at Sorrel in that damn skirt.

Emily is in the back lounge now and we're in the front. I'm glad she ain't up here. Her and her bad attitude can hide in the back all she wants.

Sorrel is smiling and having fun with the guys and my chest starts to loosen up a bit. They're playing some card game she's trying to teach them. It's called gin rummy. Johnny is getting all flustered, not able to figure it out. I sit there watching them and a grin covers my mouth. I hope this is how a majority of the tour goes.

. . .

It's officially showtime. We huddle together backstage, each of us taking a shot and doing our pre-show routine. Sorrel stands back recording us with her phone, a beaming smile on her face. The crowd is electric tonight and the vibes are high.

"How y'all doin' tonight?"

The crowd booms with cheers.

We go through the set singing each song.

"I want to sing a new song I wrote tonight for y'all."

It's Sorrel's song. It's a slower paced song but I want to give it a try.

The crowd seems to enjoy it, and no one is booing. It even looks like a few ladies have tears in their eyes. We finish the show with the last song on the set list, a faster paced song. We go over on time a little bit but no one is leaving. It feels good to be back up here. I hadn't realized how much I've missed it. Really it never mattered to me the size of the stage or the amount of the people. As long as I'm singing, I'm happy. But I still wrestle with the feeling of belonging in two different places. Part of me feels at home on stage and under the bright lights but there's something that pulls at me and makes me feel like I belong at the ranch too. I don't have time to figure out what it all means right now.

The show is finished, the lights go out, and we walk off the stage. Sorrel's waiting in the wing, eyes twinkling as she watches me. I wrap my arms around her, lifting her into the air and give her a big sweaty hug.

"How did you like it?" I ask her.

"It was amazing—I mean you were amazing! All of it. I loved it really."

"It felt really good to sing your song."

She's blushing and chewing on her bottom lip. Fuck, I can't wait to get back on the bus with her. We really haven't had any alone time and have been sharing a tiny bunk together. Her ass has been pushed up against me every night since we left and it's starting to give me blue balls.

I booked us a hotel near a couple of the venues. If I don't get her alone soon, I might lose my fucking mind.

All my post-show high flies out the window when Emily approaches us.

"Denton, we're gonna need to talk about that extra song you threw in there tonight," she retorts with a terse tone. "Boys, we have a few fans waiting for a meet and greet if you can all follow me."

Fuck her, I think.

We do the meet and greet, and by the time it's over, I'm exhausted. The boys are ready to party and I'm not sure if Sorrel wants to join them.

"Did you want to go out tonight?" I ask her.

"I'm actually pretty tired."

I sigh with relief. Groaning, I lay my head on her shoulder. "I knew we were made for each other."

She laughs and gives my head a little scratch.

When we get back to the bus, the guys get an Uber and take off to whatever country bar they can find in the city. Sorrel and I squeeze in the tiny shower together washing each other's backs, which eventually leads to me bending her over and finally the both of us get the release we've been craving.

By the time we're done, I'm ready to collapse. We snuggle up in our bunk, closing the curtain.

"I'm so happy you're here with me, baby," I tell her, pulling her in closer to me.

Softly she says, "Me too." And then she closes her eyes.

Within minutes, she's already drifted off to sleep and I'm not far behind her.

My mind is still thinking about the Emily problem, but I need to shut it off and get some rest. We'll handle it soon enough.

26

SORREL

It's been a few months now since we left for the Windsong Tour. Emily has been a pebble in my boot ever since she arrived.

If she wasn't ignoring me, then she was just being a plain old bitch. I'd had it with her and it was starting to get to me if I was being honest.

We're in Fort Worth, Texas, tonight. Denton is playing at the Dickies Arena. I'm shaking in my tiny sequin skirt with excitement because Charli is finally here with me, hence why I'm wearing a tiny sequin skirt!

Emily went into town before Charli got here and I can't fucking wait to see her reaction when she gets back. If she doesn't like me, she'll loathe Charli even more.

We're wearing matching skirts that she brought with her and tiny crop tops. I have to say Charli fills the outfit out a lot better than me with her curves and tiny frame.

She's wearing her brown curls straight tonight and I decided to curl mine. We totally look like groupies but I don't care. For Denton I am a groupie. He likes the skirt anyways; he only told me he does about five times.

Johnny was practically drooling over Charli when she got here. They had been FaceTiming every day. I asked her if she was actually into him and she got all weird and nervous. I have *never* seen her act like that over a guy. She's around cowboys all the time and never batted an eye at them, so she must have some kind of feelings for Johnny.

I'm more than okay with it. How fun would it be if they actually got together.

"Sorrel, shots—let's go!"

I take the tiny shot glass from her hand and throw back the liquor. It tastes horrible.

"What the hell was that?"

"Fireball. That's all I could find."

"Gross," I say, gagging and looking for some water. Note to self, ask what it is before I drink it.

The boys left to do sound check and rehearsals so it's just me and Charli now.

"All right, spill it Saxxon. How are you really doing?"

I sigh. "Everything's been great. It's fun but I can't lie and say I don't miss the ranch."

"I knew it," Charli says, taking a drink of her coke.

"It doesn't help that their tour manager is a raging bitch."

Just as the words fly out of my mouth, lo and behold, said tour manager walks in.

Emily puts one arm up on the doorframe and tilts her head. Her beady eyes narrow in on me. "What was that, Sorrel?"

"Um..." I have no words. I've been utterly caught.

"She said you've been a bitch."

Turning around in the booth, Charli looks Emily up and down. "What's up with that?"

Emily scoffs and does her signature eye roll.

"I don't know who the hell you are, but neither of you should be here. Denton has real talent, Sorrel, and this 'relationship' of yours is temporary. I've been in the business long enough to see how it all plays out. Trust me."

That's fucking it. It's time to stand up for myself. I've held back long enough.

"Fuck you, Emily! You have no idea what Denton and I have been through, and I don't need to prove to you how real our relationship is."

"It may be real for now but it will also be *real over* soon," she says, smirking. "I know you see all the women that throw themselves at him. He could have anyone in the world. Why would he want some nobody cowgirl whose world is so small all you know is ranch life? Don't hold him back. His world is going to be so much bigger than yours and there won't be space for you in it."

Tears begin to pool in my eyes, and Charli gives me a look and mouths, "Don't cry." I know I can't let her see me cry or she'll think she's won. But I can't help the doubt that creeps into my mind. His world is bigger than mine. I don't want a bigger world; I love the ranch and it's more than I could ever want out of this life. It makes me wonder if Denton and I are too different in that way.

His life will be award shows and music videos. Sure, I can tag along but I don't want to be famous. I don't want my picture taken at award shows and put on the internet for people to mock and judge. I never wanted any of this. I'm just a cowgirl. A cowgirl who fell for a star.

I rush past Emily as she snickers at me. I need air now. It's cold tonight and I shiver in this stupid little skirt and crop top. I feel silly now and I want the comfort of my jeans and a long-sleeve button-up. I miss the simplicity of my life. I miss not wearing makeup every day and putting my hair in a braid. Being out on the ranch, with horses and cows. I've been around people for too long.

Dash is getting homesick too. When the bus is parked, I set up a temporary pen so he can spend time outside but it isn't nearly the same freedom he has at the ranch. I've been feeling guilty for bringing him with us.

"Don't worry. I gave that bitch a piece of my mind, Sorrel. I think she's going to be acting a lot different now," Charli says as she comes down the steps of the bus. The door is still open and I'm sure Emily heard everything she said. I don't respond. I'm done fighting with Emily.

Charli slams the door shut and comes to sit in the chair next to mine.

"I think I need to go home."

"Sorrel, don't give up just yet. It's only been a couple of months."

"I'm not giving up. I just need to go home and regroup. Figure things out."

"What's there to figure out? Denton loves you. He'd do anything for you."

"That's the problem!" I say, raising my voice more than I mean to. "It's not fair to him. I'll never want this life and I can't string him along into believing I do."

"If that's what you think is right. You know I'll support you no matter what."

I have no idea what is right. My feelings are all mixed up and I don't know what to do.

"I'm going to pack. I can travel back to Montana with you tomorrow."

"If that's what you want, Sorrel," she says softly.

By the look on her face, she thinks I'm making the wrong choice but I've made up my mind.

I pack my things and hide my suitcase in Charli's truck. I'm happy she decided to drive instead of fly. She was visiting family here in Texas so it worked out perfectly when the tour landed in Fort Worth. I hope Denton doesn't think I was planning this all along. I won't tell him I'm leaving until after the show. I know if I do it before it will ruin his night.

Tears prick my eyes and I swipe them away quickly. The sound of laughter and Denton's voice, coming toward us. I plaster on my best smile, shaking away my anger.

"Hey, babe."

I give Denton a quick peck and he gives me a confused look.

"Break a leg tonight or whatever they say," I laugh nervously.

"What's wrong, Sorrel?"

"Nothing!" I say quickly. "Everything's great. It looks like you got a great crowd tonight. I'm excited for you."

Damn, I hate how he can sense something's wrong. It's like he's studied my emotions and notices the slightest shift.

"Yeah…it'll be a good time. You seen Emily? She left rehearsal early."

"She's in the back lounge I think."

I'm annoyed he's looking for her. Who cares where she is? I wish she'd go back to whatever bitch hole she crawled out of. Denton leaves to go find her and I join the others.

Charli has a cheesy grin on her face as her and Johnny banter back and forth relentlessly. They're perfect for each other. I'm happy for her but sad for myself, dreading the conversation I know I'll be having with Denton in the morning. I'll do my best not to think about it tonight. My best friend is here and I want her to have a fun night in her old stomping grounds.

. . .

Charli and I hang out backstage with our new friends. the Lone Star Revival band who opened for Denton. The lead singer is a fiery redhead but she's as sweet as can be. Her voice is rustic and sweet like honey all at the same time. She was amazing during her performance. She grew up on a ranch here in Fort Worth Texas so we have that in common and it's nice to be able to talk with someone who gets it.

"So how long have you and Denton been together?"

"Oh, uh, a couple of months. We were friends before we started dating though. He basically forced me into a friendship with him when he showed up at my family's ranch over the summer," I joke.

"No way! That's the cutest love story ever. He better write a song about it if he hasn't already."

I smile knowingly. I watch as her and Charli go to the bar to take shots. I'm not in the mood for partying anymore but I'm trying my best to rally. It's probably best if one of us stays sober anyways. Someone's gotta be the responsible one of the group.

Denton is up now and we head over to the right wing. Johnny takes his spot and blows a kiss to Charli and she catches it and puts it to her lips. I shake my head and laugh at how cringy they are. Denton turns his head to me and gives me a tight smile. I try to give him one back but my heart hurts knowing I'm leaving.

I scan the backstage area looking for the harsh tour manager, but Emily is nowhere to be found. Now she isn't even doing her job. Jake really needs to do a better job at checking credentials before hiring these people.

The concert is almost over and the energy is strange. The crowd doesn't buzz with their usual electricity. Denton's vibe is off and his heart isn't in it tonight—it reflects in the crowd.

I know it's not fair to the people who paid to watch him. Hopefully they understand that he's a real human who has bad nights too. I think when people watch performers it's like they almost forget we're just like them. We have emotions and our feelings get hurt too. We're not robots who were made to entertain people. But ultimately that settles it for me. I can't be a distraction for him anymore.

27

DENTON

I was so off tonight and the audience was feeding off my energy. Johnny and Grady kept making eye contact with me and I can tell they're pissed. I just can't get out of this funk no matter how hard I try.

I fired Emily right before the show. I was done with her shit and I don't care that we won't have a tour manager. We don't need her anymore. We did it all ourselves before. I'm sure we'll make it work.

I know that's why Sorrel is being odd. Emily has been picking on her since the start of the tour. I'm sure having Charli here stirred up more drama.

During the entire show, all I could think about was wanting to talk to Sorrel and figure out what was going through that beautiful mind of hers.

It wasn't just Sorrel though. I'm already feeling burnout approaching and we're only a couple months into this tour. Maybe I got too used to living a slower life. Doesn't matter though, I've gotta see it through. I signed a contract and there's no getting out of this.

Ticket sales have been great, and our fans are amazing—I really shouldn't be complaining. There're a thousand other artists that would kill to be in our position. I feel guilt-ridden for even feeling this way.

When I sang the last song on the set list, I walked right off the stage. No autographs or goodbyes. I had to get out of there—out of the spotlight.

My chest feels tight and my breathing is shallow. I rush past everyone standing around back stage, including Sorrel. I can't be around anyone right now.

I make it to my dressing room and slam the door shut. Sinking to the floor and slamming my head against the wall, I try to catch my breath. What the fuck is this? A damn panic attack?

I haven't had one since I was a kid. The last one was when my mom and dad got into a huge fight and I tried to break it up. I was a lot smaller back then and he threw us both around like rag dolls. I remember feeling so hopeless—he was so much bigger than me—there was nothing I could do to stop him. My mom found me in my bedroom curled up in a ball in the midst of a full-blown panic attack. I remember thinking I was dying. I recognize the signs now, so I know I'm not having a heart attack.

There's a soft knock at the door.

"Denton?" I hear Sorrel's sweet voice behind the door.

I try to breathe and get the words out. "Come—" *Gasp.* "In."

She slowly opens the door, peeking her head in first.

"Oh my gosh, are you okay?"

"Yeah, I'm fine," I say through shortened breaths. I attempt a fake smile, but she ain't buying it.

Sorrel's eyes are dark with worry. I can tell by the stiff way she's holding herself she doesn't know what to do. She's scared to touch me. I open up my arm inviting her to come sit next to me. She hesitates and then slowly sits down like I'm a rabid animal who might attack at any moment.

"It's just a panic attack," I say, reassuring her. "It'll pass." My voice is gravel as I try to get the words out.

"Can I get you anything?"

"No, just sit here with me please."

I wanted to be alone but I actually feel better having her here. She matches her breathing to mine and we both take in long deep breaths slowly letting them out.

"I'm sorry you have to see me like this."

"Denton, don't ever be sorry for that. It just proves you're human."

I chuckle at that. "Yeah, that easy confidence thing I try to portray isn't always the case," I admit to her.

It's part of my job to be confident and portray a certain look. Sorrel sees the real me. The ugly, the doubt, the fear, hesitation, all of it.

I look at her. "Are you leaving me?"

I don't know why I ask her that. Something in my gut just tells me she is.

She looks down at her lap, brows knitting. "I'm going home with Charli tomorrow."

I just nod. I don't fight her on it because I get it. If I could go back to what she has, I would too. It breaks my heart but I understand.

"It's not why you think."

"You don't have to explain yourself, Sorrel. I get it."

"Yes, I do. You deserve to know why. Emily, she was right—"

I practically growl when I hear her mention her name.

"Don't you dare listen to a fucking thing that chick says. I fired her before the show tonight."

Her brows fly up to her forehead. "You did?"

"Yeah, I wanted her gone the first day she stepped foot on our bus. We're out a tour manager now but we'll make do. I'll just have a little more on my plate."

She shakes her head in disbelief.

"If that's the reason you're leaving—"

"It's not," she says, cutting me off. "Well, it's part of it, but it's not the only reason. I've loved being here with you but I miss my simple life back at the ranch. I don't want to hold you back or be a distraction." She pauses, then continues on. "Denton, these people love you. Your shows get bigger each city we're in. You're a star and I'm just a cowgirl who lives a quiet life and that's all I want."

"I want that too. I mean I'm grateful for all of this and it's what I've always dreamed of, but now that I have it, I'm not sure anymore."

"You can't just walk away from this."

I run my hands through my hair in frustration. "No, I can't, but there's gotta be some middle ground."

"What do you mean?"

"I'm not sure just yet but I'll figure it out. If going home is what you need, Sorrel, don't let me hold you back."

She purses her lips. "Okay, so I guess that's it then. I'm going home."

I bite my tongue. It's not fair of me to ask her to stay. I don't want to say the wrong thing either and make her feel worse than I know she already does.

"Let's head back to the bus," I tell her, taking her hand in mine as we stand up.

—

The next morning Johnny and Charli come rolling into the bus—smiles beaming and all over each other. Well at least someone had a good night.

I let Sorrel have the bunk to herself and I slept on the couch. She had been distant once we got back on the bus and I wanted to give her space and time to think. I needed the same. Just because she's leaving doesn't mean this is over between us. It will just take a little more effort on both our ends. Relationships are give and take, right?

The rest of her bags are sitting by the door and Dash is curled up on top of one of them. There's no way he's getting left behind. I'll miss that little guy. I enjoyed having our little mascot while we were on tour. He even got to come out on stage at one of the smaller shows when we were in Oklahoma.

Sorrel is already dressed and ready to leave. Her hair is in a long braid and she has on a ball cap, tank top, and her usual jeans. She looks gorgeous as always in an effortless kind of way.

"You about ready to hit the road?" Charli calls out to Sorrel. She's sitting on Johnny's lap, sipping on an iced coffee.

"Yeah, just about—Denton, can we talk before I leave?"

I rush over to her. "Yeah, of course. Let's go outside."

She follows me out and we sit in the two lounge chairs set up. She has already taken down Dash's pen. Rubbing her hands down her pants, she says, "I'm sorry this didn't work out, Denton."

I take both her hands into mine. "Hey, look at me."

Her blue eyes are glossy as she does. "Don't worry. It's going to be okay. We'll make it work," I tell her.

"What do you mean? I thought last night—you said—I mean I thought we were done."

"What? No, I mean I'm not done. Unless you are?"

My shoulders drop and my head falls down to the floor. I feel actual tears in the back of my eyes. Is this it? Is she breaking up with me?

I pictured forever with her. I feel sick to my stomach and a million thoughts run through my mind. I can't imagine my life without her now. But if she doesn't want me, then there's nothing I can do.

28

SORREL

I assumed last night when I said, "I guess this is it," and Denton didn't say anything back, we were over.

He slept on the couch and I cried all night in our bunk. I don't know how he didn't notice how puffy my eyes and face were this morning. I got up before him and took a cold shower to try and numb the pain of it all. Every time I tried to put on my makeup, tears would start falling. Now he's telling me it's not over and I don't know what to think.

It looks like he's crying now and it makes me cry even more. We're both sitting here crying, and when he finally looks back up at me, we hold each other's gaze.

I don't know why but a smile starts to tug at his lips and I let out a strangled laugh—wiping the snot from my nose with the back of my hand. Now we're both laughing and crying at the same time. What the fuck is wrong with us?

"I don't want to be done. I just thought last night we were when you didn't say anything or come to bed."

"I'm sorry. I thought you wanted space."

"No, I wanted you. Clearly, we need to work on our communication skills," I say, letting out a light laugh.

Sniffling and wiping at his nose, he says, "Yeah, I think you're right."

We take a moment to compose ourselves.

His eyes darken and his tone turns serious. "Sorrel, miles don't break what's meant to last."

And my heart aches all over again, in a good way.

"Whether we're hundreds or thousands of miles apart it will never change the love I have for you."

I crawl into his arms and he touches his forehead to mine.

"I love you," I say breathlessly.

"I love you too, baby."

My heart grows in my chest and I'm relieved that he still wants to make it work. I know a good thing when I see it, and even if I don't get to see it nearly enough, it will all be worth it.

Charli and Johnny come out of the bus.

"Did you two kiss and make up or what?" Johnny says and Charli elbows him in the side "Ow, that hurt," he says to her, pouting.

I roll my eyes at him.

"Everything's all good." Denton says, smiling down at me. "Just working out a few kinks is all."

"Yay!" Charli squeals running over to hug us both.

We hug her back and laugh.

"So, you still coming home?"

"Yes, she is. She belongs at the ranch but she'll be taking my heart with her when she goes," Denton tells Charli.

"Damn, you've gotten cheesy," Johnny says to Denton, and Charli shoots him another look.

"We're going to try the long-distance thing for a little while," I say.

"Not try. We're gonna do it and we'll figure it out from there. Honestly, I want to be at the ranch as bad as she does," Denton says.

"I guess you are a real cowboy," Johnny says, patting Denton on the shoulder. "It's part of your life now."

We all smile at him, being sincere and not being sarcastic for once.

"It is. I'm not giving up on singing, but I have some decisions to make about my career."

I thought I was the reason he was hesitant about where his career was going and how it was taking off but from what he's saying it sounds like it isn't only because of me. That's a huge relief because I don't want to be the reason he doesn't follow through on anything. Then in twenty years he resents me for holding him back from being a huge star. Even still, I won't let him give up on his dreams. Whatever they may be now. He was there for me when I needed him and I'll be here for him. Even if that means steering him in the right direction.

"I know somehow I can have the best of both

worlds. The ranch and music. I've just got to figure it out."

I smile and nod, "I'll support you in any way I can babe," I tell him.

"I know you will, darlin'."

We say our goodbyes and I cry all over again. Gosh, I'm going to dry up from losing so many tears. Denton picks up Dash and gives him a few scratches behind his ears.

"I'm gonna miss you, buddy, but I'll miss your mama even more."

I take Dash from him and put him in the front seat. Charli is already in the driver's seat and the engine of her diesel truck is roaring. Her and Johnny's goodbyes weren't nearly as emotional. They're more in the hot and heavy phase, unable to keep their hands off each other.

"Well, I'll see you soon?" I ask Denton.

"You will. I'll figure out a way to come see you even if we have to move some things around. I love you, Sorrel Saxxon."

"I love you too, Denton Reed," I say, getting on my tippy-toes to kiss him goodbye.

He holds me in a firm and long embrace and our mouths come together—tongue and all. I can't get enough and I want to remember the way he tastes. Fuck, this is going to be hard.

We finally pull apart when Charli honks her horn. I leave without turning around and I can feel him watching me as I climb into the pickup. When we finally drive off, I look back through the rear windshield and he's still standing there watching us. He gives me a small wave and I give him one back as a stray tear slides down my cheek.

We get on the highway and begin the twenty-hour drive back to the Saxxon Ranch. *Home.*

It's been nearly five months since I left Fort Worth to go home, back to the Saxxon Ranch. Right after I left, Denton moved around a few shows and was able to fly out and spend four days at the ranch. I traveled to him the next time and met him in Telluride, Colorado, around Christmas to meet his mom and sister.

We all stayed in a cabin together and went snowboarding, drank hot chocolate, and played cards by the fire every night. It was a blast. They're spending a week at the ranch with us this summer and we can't wait.

Denton has a show in Arizona tomorrow night, and the Cave Creek pro rodeo is the same weekend so Charli and I decided to enter. I love the cold Montana winter, but this Arizona sun sure does feel good.

I was starting to go stir crazy in my cabin. When he said he was going to be on the west coast until spring, I jumped at the opportunity to enter a few pro rodeos out west. Charli and I made the long haul to Arizona and we've been here for a few days now. We have a blast traveling and entering rodeos together.

Charli is almost up to run and I can hear Johnny

whooping and hollering from the stands. They're still paired up and it makes it easier that we can both complain about our long-distance relationships.

Johnny got to Arizona early and had booked him and Charli a romantic date night. It was fucking adorable. I felt like I was her dad when I answered his knock on the trailer door, here to pick her up. I even played the tough guy act and everything. Told him to have her home by eleven. Let's just say she never came home that night.

I'm mounted on Duke and we're sitting behind the arena fence, waiting our turn to run. I take it all in, the fans in the bleachers, vendors set up selling hats, tack, and more. The smell of fresh kettle corn in the air. Kids are playing and roping dummies, some of them with a rope in their hand for the first time. I love this way of life. I couldn't imagine it any other way.

Charli's up to run now. She's running her mare Dolly. She's a short and stocky buckskin mare, who's wicked fast. They look badass, storming into the arena. Charli pushes her hard to the first barrel and she slips a little getting around it. Fuck, that will cost them some time. It doesn't faze them though. She's bent over the saddle horn, arms out and legs kicking to the next barrel. Their last two barrels are clean and she pushes her mare home. What a great run.

Duke and I trot over to them as she cools Dolly off.

"Fuck yeah, good run!" I tell her.

"Thanks, babe, your turn. Turn and burn, baby!"

I chuckle and pull my hat down on my head—making my way toward the arena entrance.

Just like every time I run, my stomach twists and Duke can feel the anticipation. He's prancing and rearing and I have to hold him back until the buzzer sounds. It goes off and I send him forward.

Riding him is like being on autopilot. He knows his job so well—I just have to stay out of his way. I hear someone cheering me on from the stands, which I normally try to tune out but that voice is familiar. It motivates me and I push Duke hard running home. We have a good run and I'm excited to see where we'll end up when the weekend is over.

I cool Duke off in the back arena slowing to a trot and eventually a walk. A tall handsome cowboy is walking toward us and my chest twists when his face comes into focus.

My Denton. His smile is so big I can make out that one dimple that rarely makes an appearance. He's got a little scruff on his chiseled jaw and he's wearing a felt cowboy hat and my favorite Wrangler denim pearl-snap shirt. Damn, he looks good.

A happy little squeal comes out of me as I jump off Duke and run to where he's now standing at the fence. I climb onto the bottom pole and lean over and give him a kiss. Duke starts nickering when he realizes who it is and I laugh.

"Even Duke missed you!"

"Well, hello, to you too gorgeous," he says, giving me that smile that heats me to my core every time.

"I didn't think you were gonna make it in time to see my run."

"Ray was pedal to the floor the whole way here. I told him if we missed your run, he was gonna get an ear full from Charli. That kicked him into high gear." He chuckles.

I smile down at him and go in for more kisses. We need to get back to my trailer before someone says something about too much PDA. I can't help myself though I'm so happy he's here.

"Let's get back to my trailer. Dash is going to go crazy when he sees you."

I lead Duke out of the arena, loosening his cinch before we leave. Denton gives him a few scratches on his withers.

He comes to my left side and we hold hands walking through the rows of trailers, passing cowboys and cowgirls. I can tell a few of them recognize Denton but they leave us be.

When we make it back to my trailer, I hurry and unsaddle Duke. Denton helps and throws some hay in his portable pen and fills his water.

"Thanks, babe," I beam at him.

I let Dash out of the trailer now that Duke is put up and he literally howls in excitement jumping up and down for Denton to pick him up. He's laughing and takes him into his arms.

"You're such a good dog dad," I joke.

"Hopefully that means I'll be a good human dad too," he says softly.

My heart leaps into my throat when I think about

him and babies. Hopefully my babies, which would be our babies. I need to get him in the trailer now.

I grab his hand and pull him to the door.

"I'm comin', cowgirl, slow down." He laughs.

I struggle with the buttons on my shirt.

"Go lay down, We need some alone time," I tell Dash.

29

DENTON

I'm sweating bullets, getting ready for our show tonight. I have a tingly sensation all over my body that won't go away and I think my central nervous system is about to shut down.

Sorrel and I had an amazing night after her run. We made love, cooked food with some of their rodeo friends, and hung out all night sitting in a circle sipping on long necks and telling cowboy stories. I'm feeling more inspired than ever. I have so many ideas for new songs in my head it feels like it's going to explode.

I can't focus on that right now though because we're about to play one of our biggest shows ever. Tonight's venue is the Talking Stick Resort Amphitheatre in Phoenix, Arizona. There'll be twenty thousand people watching us perform. I want everything to be perfect, which is the reason I'm so damned nervous.

It's eighty fucking degrees here today and it's only

February. I can't imagine living here in the summer. I don't know how Sophia and her family do it. We invited them to the show tonight with free tickets. Sophia really grew on Sorrel. It's sweet and I love how she's such a good role model for young cowgirls.

I invited a few other people that Sorrel doesn't know about. I think the surprise I have for her tonight is going to top the time I showed up at her family's ranch uninvited. I smile to myself thinking about it and look down at my watch to check the time. One hour until showtime.

"You ready for this?" Parker asks me and I nod.

"He fucking better be ready. This is serious shit!" Johnny butts in.

I know I'm ready. Hell, I've been ready since the first time I told her I loved her. I just hope she is too.

"Well, I hope she is or this is gonna be really fucking embarrassing."

Grady gives Johnny a dirty look. "She is," he says.

I'm thankful for Grady and his good sense. We'd all be so screwed without him.

"Thanks, Grady." I say, giving him an appreciative grin.

Sorrel and Charli should be here soon. I wasn't sure if I should see her before just in case I give something away, but she might be suspicious if we don't all hang out on the bus before the show like usual. She said her and Charli were going to watch the last perf at the rodeo and then get ready and drive out this way.

We're done with soundcheck now and everything has been running so much smoother now that we have our new tour manager Cash. He's in his mid-forties, country type of guy, and he fits in great. When I told him what I wanted to do for tonight, he was all for it. He helped me plan everything out.

I'm rushing back to the bus now to shower and get ready before the gals get here. I'm already sweating again when I get out of the shower. Fuck, I guess it is what it is.

I put on Sorrel's favorite shirt, my denim pearl-snap and my gray felt cowboy hat. I got a haircut, trimmed my scruff, and I think I look half way decent.

"Honey, I'm home!" I hear Sorrel's voice call out from the front of the bus.

Here comes that tingly feeling again and I think I might pass out.

I shake it off and stride over to her, picking her up in my arms and giving her a big kiss on the mouth.

"You look amazing, darlin'."

She really does. She has on a short white mini dress, her nicer pair of boots, and her hair is in soft curls that flow over her shoulders. She already looks like a bride and I'd marry her just like this.

"Thanks, honey, so do you. That's my favorite shirt, you know."

I clear my throat. "Yeah, I know. Drinks?" I need something strong and need it bad.

"I'll make 'em." She starts rummaging through the liquor cabinet and pulls out the bottle of Crown.

She goes to the fridge and grabs a can of Sprite and some cranberry juice.

The rest of the group pile into the bus now, and she makes enough drinks for everyone.

"Look at you getting all fancy with those drinks," Charli says to her.

Sorrel smiles and I just stand there watching her mesmerized. I'm still as enamored with her as the first time I ever saw her. A chill goes down my spine when I think in just a few short hours she'll hopefully be my fiancée.

We all gather around and cheers.

"To our biggest show yet, let's fucking go!" Johnny calls out, and we all toast to that.

"Time to go, babe. I'll see you out there," I say, leaning over and giving her a kiss on her cheek goodbye. I take a handful of her ass too. I can't help myself in that damn dress.

"Hey!" She giggles, swatting my hand away. "Go kill it, baby!"

I'm quiet as we head to the stage.

"You gonna be like this all night?" Johnny asks me.

"No, just nervous is all. Maybe I shouldn't be doing this in front of all these people."

I planned on asking her alone at our spot by the waterfall, but it never worked out and I couldn't wait any longer. I wanted Sorrel to be my wife yesterday. I'm so ready to start our lives together as husband and wife. We'd figure everything else out along the way.

"Hey, guys! You all look great!" It's Cash. He has

a bottle of Pendleton whiskey in his hands and he holds it out to me. "Denton, I thought you might need this."

Good man, I think and open the bottle taking a swig. A little liquid courage—I'm ready to put on the show of my life and get me a wife.

EPILOGUE

Six months ago, Denton Reed proposed to me at his show in Phoenix, Arizona, in front of twenty thousand people. I of course said yes to him.

When he sang my song and changed the lyrics to "I'm going to give you a ring" my heart leaped out of my fucking chest. He called me onto the stage—I was so nervous but I'd been in front of huge crowds before. I told myself, *It's just like a rodeo.*

When I got to center stage with him, I saw my whole family was in the pit right up front. Mom and Sable, Dad, Sutton, Ryder, and Trotter. I couldn't believe it. Seeing all of them there had already made me start to cry, but when he got down on one knee and asked me to marry him, I lost it. It was the best night of our lives.

When we checked into our VRBO in Cave Creek, Arizona, the next day, Charli and my family surprised us with an engagement party.

The place was beautiful—settled into the mountains and surrounded by the Arizona desert. It was so different than Montana but no less beautiful as the sky was painted orange and pink that night. Everyone was there, Denton's family and mine, along with some of our closest friends. I was shocked to find out Dad and Sutton left the ranch in charge to Walker. But I think it was a good excuse for everyone to get away from the frigid Montana winter for a little while. My heart felt like it was going to overflow with love that night.

IT'S SUMMER AGAIN HERE AT THE RANCH. THE guesthouse is full—Denton's mom and sister, my mom, Sable—everyone's all here. It's been so fun working on wedding planning, dress shopping, and they're throwing me a bridal shower soon. Even Sutton is helping out. We're having a winter wedding this year. It's fast, but Denton was ready to get married yesterday, and I can confidently say I'm more than ready too.

His tour is almost over. He's decided to take the next year off and has booked gigs every weekend at the Wagon Wheel. The band is going to be living in the bunkhouses with the ranch hands. Maybe we'll make real cowboys of them after all.

I'm sitting outside overlooking the ranch on the porch swing.

"What's going through that pretty head of yours, my sweet fiancée?" Denton asks me.

"Honestly?"

He looks at me like I should know better.

"I was just thinking back to how we got here. I was wondering if we didn't go through everything we had with Kenzington, would we be where we are today?"

"And?" Denton says.

"I don't think we would. I think in a way it brought us together. I think maybe that's what really brings people together. Challenges."

"I get that. But I'm glad we haven't had anymore *challenges*," he quips.

We rock back and forth in that familiar silence, just like we always have, Dash curled in my lap and my head tucked into Denton's chest.

I think I'm done with challenges too.

Huck Kenzington's trial is scheduled at the end of this year. I'm still deciding whether I want to attend it. I've closed that chapter of my life. I've healed from the trauma he caused. And with the help of Denton, I broke down my walls and I feel more alive than ever.

I love the person I've become with him. They say there's something about working on yourself alone, but what about growing together? That's exactly what we've done. Two people—both flawed—but evolving, navigating challenges together, and continuing to become better versions of ourselves each and every day. Now that's true love.

ACKNOWLEDGMENTS

Thank you to my wonderful husband for always supporting my dreams.

Thank you to my family and friends for all of your support.

COMING SOON

Book Two in the Saxxon Ranch Series… Stay tuned for Sutton and Ryder Saxxon's love story.

ABOUT THE AUTHOR

Sierra Mac was born and raised in Arizona. Her, her husband and their two dogs reside in a quaint little desert town with one gas station and a bar that does live bull riding on Thursdays and Saturdays.

Her love for the western industry started when she was seventeen years old. She moved to Prescott, Arizona, where she studied equine and began taking horseback riding lessons.

With a love for writing and stories to tell, she decided to combine her two greatest passions.

She plans to write more cowboy romance novels in the future.

www.ingramcontent.com/pod-product-compliance
Lightning Source LLC
LaVergne TN
LVHW091148150826
845672LV00005B/1070

* 9 7 9 8 9 9 5 4 7 5 3 0 9 *